SO-CEZ-753

Mollie Molay

MARRIAGE BY MISTAKE

Harlequin Books

TORONTO • NEW YORK • LONDON
AMSTERDAM • PARIS • SYDNEY • HAMBURG
STOCKHOLM • ATHENS • TOKYO • MILAN
MADRID • WARSAW • BUDAPEST • AUCKLAND

For my daughters, Elaine Fox and Joy Steinhardt, whose
love and devotion have made the road easier.
And to the memory of their father, Louis Matza, who
taught me that anything worth doing is worth doing well.

ISBN 0-373-16616-8

MARRIAGE BY MISTAKE

"It was a proxy marriage...wasn't it?"

Judge Potter sighed. "You're asking me?"

"Yes, well, I know it sounds strange, but—" Jon hesitated "—the little lady's nervous you didn't say the word 'proxy' in the ceremony."

A frown creased the elderly man's face and he stroked his beard. "Married at least five couples today.... Say, yours was a strange wedding, wasn't it? Never did see such a reluctant bride. Still, she is your wife."

"That's the point, Your Honor. Alex was just standing in for the bride."

"You don't say? Well, things got a little confusing in there, you must admit." He eyed Jon briefly before he continued. "Well, looks like I might've married you to the wrong woman, doesn't it?"

ABOUT THE AUTHOR

 Mollie Molay started writing years ago when, as a going-away present, her co-workers gave her an electric typewriter. Since then, she's gone on to sell three novels and become president of the Los Angeles Romance Writers of America. A part-time travel agent, Mollie spends her spare time volunteering; she's grateful for her good fortune and wants to give back to those around her.

Books by Mollie Molay

HARLEQUIN AMERICAN ROMANCE
560—FROM DRIFTER TO DADDY
597—HER TWO HUSBANDS

Chapter One

"Do you, Stacey Arden, take this man to be your lawfully wedded husband, to have and to hold, for richer or for poorer, in sickness and in health till death do you part?"

Alex panicked at the question. Never mind that her name wasn't Stacey Arden, nor that she'd only met the bridegroom a scant two hours ago, she *felt* like a bride. Scenes from an earlier time and place flashed before her eyes.

The expected reply froze in her throat. She didn't *want* to feel like a bride! That wasn't what she was here for. As she hesitated, she was uncomfortably aware that the justice of the peace and the man standing at her side were waiting for her answer.

They couldn't be expected to know she'd been a bride before—almost. That she'd waited in another courtroom for over an hour, under pitying glances, before she'd realized she'd been stood up by the groom. Granted, the man beside her now was going through with his marriage vows, but he wasn't actually going to be her husband. In a few minutes, he'd say goodbye and she'd be left alone again.

At her continued silence, the groom, Jon Waring, glanced down at her in surprise. Eyes wide, she gazed back. For a quick moment, she was afraid she was going to faint.

"Are you okay?" he asked, reaching for Alex's arm to steady her.

Alex swallowed the lump in her throat. "I'm not sure."

"You don't have to go through with this, if it bothers you that much," he finally said. "I'll find someone else."

The justice of the peace, Homer Potter, frowned at the groom's comment. Before he could speak, Alex forced herself to rein in her memories. This was just a proxy marriage, after all. And she had volunteered to be the proxy bride.

"No. It's all right. I'll stay." She owed the man something for his money.

He nodded, his relief apparent. "Go ahead, Your Honor."

Potter peered over his glasses at Alex. "Let the little lady speak for herself. Are you sure you want to proceed, young woman?"

"I guess so." Alex felt foolish. She smiled apologetically at the justice of the peace.

"You guess so?" Potter rocked back on his heels.

The court clerk and the two cleaning ladies who'd been roped in as witnesses lost their encouraging smiles.

Alex took a deep breath. "I'm ready."

Potter obliged. "In sickness and in health till death do you part?" he repeated.

"I do," Alex said firmly.

The elderly official beamed. The witnesses squealed. The groom took her cold hand and put a shiny new gold wedding band on her icy third finger, left hand. Dimly she heard Potter say, "I now pronounce you man and wife. You may kiss the bride."

Alex blinked. She'd never anticipated having to kiss the groom. She fidgeted, gazed down at the floor, at the plastic plants that had been brought in to doll up the courtroom—anywhere but at Jon Waring. Well, the sooner she let him follow Potter's instructions, the sooner she'd be out of here. She raised her head and waited for the groom to make the next move.

He leaned forward and aimed a light kiss at her cheek. Instinctively—or was it because she'd wondered if he kissed as good as he looked?—she turned her lips to meet his.

The kiss took her by surprise. As if he were as curious about her as she was about him, the token kiss became something more. His lips lingered on hers, urged her to respond. And respond she did. When her lips had instinctively parted under his, she was shocked by the tingle of awareness that swept through her.

She opened her eyes and flushed at the odd expression on the groom's face. "I didn't mean to do that. I don't know what got into me."

"That's okay. I know it was only a kiss to seal the bargain," he reassured her with a knowing smile. "And to keep Potter happy. Right?"

She had a strange feeling it had turned out to be more than that.

Alex squirmed. The man obviously thought the whole thing was amusing. She didn't. If she had been made of sterner stuff, she would have offered him her cheek to kiss. She hadn't been able to, not when he was her idea of a real man—and very masculine in his tailored Western wedding finery. Tall, ruggedly handsome, there was an aura of strength and sensuality about him that drew her in spite of herself.

His reassuring smile as he looked down at her did nothing to calm her confusion. She could hardly believe how much she responded to him. After all, she hardly knew him. What was fate doing to her, putting this man in her life when all she wanted was a story for a human interest column she intended to write?

Her lips still tingled from the obligatory kiss he'd given her. His lips had been warm and his skin, as it brushed her cheek, soft. His breath had smelled of cinnamon-laced coffee, his shaving lotion of mountain air and green trees. For a crazy moment, she wondered what it would be like to actually be his wife. Goodness, what was she thinking of? The man was already taken. Besides, he was a cowboy, or some sort of macho man. Not her kind at all.

His voice, and his murmured thank-you as they turned to leave the courtroom, sent a spark of physical awareness through her. Damn, of all the men she could have drawn as a subject for a story, why did it have to be someone who could have changed her mind about not wanting to be a blushing bride?

She firmly reminded herself that she wasn't ready to be a bride, anyway. She had a career to pursue, dreams to live.

"Wait up, young man. There's papers to be signed."

Alex looked back to see Justice Potter beckoning to them. She rolled her eyes in disbelief at the man who looked like Doc in the *Seven Dwarfs,* beard and all. No reader would ever believe this story!

"Sorry. I guess it's not over yet." The groom held out his hand. "Do you mind . . . ?" He led her back to the table in front of the justice's bench, took the wedding certificate from the beaming clerk and quickly signed on the appropriate line. He waited for her to take her turn.

Alex quickly entered her name at the spot Potter indicated and made for the door with Jon at her heels.

Potter's judicial voice floated after them. "Good luck, folks. I hope today will be the start of a happy life together."

Alex was puzzled by his comment. He seemed to be under the impression she and Jon Waring were actually man and wife. If the man only knew the real reason she was here.

Outside in the corridor, Jon caught her by the arm. "Thank you again, Miss Storm. I know you were uncomfortable back there. Do you mind telling me why you went through with the ceremony?"

This wasn't the time to tell him the truth. That when she'd seen his ad in the personals offering five hundred dollars and expenses to a proxy bride, all she thought was what a great human interest story it would make. She'd done a lot of strange things in her life, but she didn't think he'd appreciate her motives. As it was, he probably thought she was here only because she needed the money. Not that she couldn't use it, but she needed the story more.

Alex said the first thing that came to mind. "It sounded like fun."

"Fun?"

"Yes, in a romantic sort of way." Alex flushed as she realized how inane she must sound. She shifted her purse to her other shoulder and yanked at the skirt of her rose-colored suit—the new short length was decidedly inconvenient, she thought as she wiggled to straighten the lacy minislip that threatened to wrap itself around her waist. For a would-be journalist, she wasn't doing too well at sounding professional.

"You were acting as if your life was threatened," Jon went on. "I'd hardly call that romantic."

Alex took a deep breath. That was exactly how she *had* felt when the judge had asked her if she took this man to be her wedded husband—threatened.

"Well..." She hesitated. How could she explain her panic to a total stranger? Pride prevented her from telling him about being stood up at the altar almost five years ago. "It's just that I have this thing about getting married, and I was beginning to feel like a real bride. I guess I should apologize for my behavior."

"That's okay," Jon said, "I was feeling kind of strange there for a moment myself." For him, it had been the knowledge that, in addition to taking a wife, he was about to become a father, too. A status he'd avoided until now as a threat to his wanderlust and independence. He wasn't sure he was ready for either one, but a commitment was a commitment. As for his proxy bride, he suspected she had a few hang-ups of her own.

A slight frown creased his forehead as he glanced down at her suit, an inexpensive copy of the latest Chanel. "I still don't know why you wanted to be a proxy bride. Unless, of course, it was just a matter of the money."

"Not exactly," she replied, "but it will come in handy."

Whatever the reason, Jon was glad she'd decided to go through with the agreement. When he'd met her for the first time at her hotel, the promise of the soft, sweet voice he'd heard over the phone had been fulfilled. Her curly dark brown hair framed luminescent hazel eyes in a face a man would kill for. It had been all of that, and now, her gutsy determination to see her bargain through. For a moment his admiration for her made him forget Stacey, his real wife, until guilt overtook him.

Getting married hadn't been his A-1 priority. Reluctantly becoming a father was, but it seemed he couldn't have one without the other. Difficult, when his intended bride had had to leave before the wedding ceremony.

As he gazed down at Alex, he had to remind himself this was the woman who had stood in for Stacey. A very reluctant proxy bride, as it had turned out.

He eyed Alex, his interest disguised as nonchalance. "Well, I'll keep my side of the bargain," he said, digging his wallet out of his jacket and handing her five one-hundred-dollar bills. "Here you go. And thanks."

He blinked at the expression on her face.

"What's the matter? Isn't it enough?"

"More than enough. Especially since you sent me the airplane tickets. Actually, I would have settled for the story."

At Jon's sharp intake of breath, Alex flushed. Damn, she'd never make it as a journalist if she couldn't keep her mouth shut. That was supposed to be a secret. What was there about this man that made her tell him the truth?

"What story?"

"This quaint proxy wedding stuff. It's going to be the background material for a human interest story I intend to write."

"A reporter? I don't believe it!" His gaze grew cold, his lips tight with anger. "Why couldn't you have told me the truth?"

"Because I was afraid you'd react this way." Ready to leave, if necessary, Alex took a step away from him.

"You're not going to write about this marriage!" The threat in his voice was clear.

"Of course I am."

"No, you're not!"

"Come on, Mr. Waring." She gave him her best smile. "Don't be a bad sport."

"It's *my* life you want to write about." His brows snapped together, her attraction for him forgotten. Damn! If word of a proxy marriage got out, his plans would be jeopardized. He should have screened her more carefully. "You never said anything before about being a reporter. If you had, I never would have hired you.''

''I'm not a reporter. I hope to be a published journalist someday. I intend to write human interest stories. Besides, what difference does it make? With my luck,'' she muttered as she gazed defiantly back at him, ''the story may never reach the newspapers.''

''A lot!''

''I resent that. What do you have against journalists?'' Alex drew herself up to her full five feet two inches.

''Not a thing. At least, not until now.'' The disgusted tone in his voice said it all.

The proxy marriage, legal here in Montana, had become necessary when Stacey Arden, an international journalist, had been recalled to Europe for a breaking story. Since it turned out she didn't know when she'd be able to return, he'd had to act fast to find a proxy. But he'd never dreamed he'd find someone who could blast his plans to hell.

''Excuse me,'' a deep voice bellowed behind them. ''It's bad luck to quarrel on your wedding day.''

Jon fixed Alex with a quelling look and turned to see Justice Potter standing above them on the steps of the courthouse.

''For a newly married couple, you folks seem to have difficulty getting along. Sure you don't want to go back in and call the whole thing off?''

''No, thanks,'' Jon said with a warning glance at Alex.

"Just thought I'd lighten up the situation, folks."
Potter waved to a passing attorney and went back up
the steps.

Alex stared after him. "What did he mean, 'for a
newly married couple'? This *was* a proxy marriage,
wasn't it?"

Jon eyed her in disgust. "Of course, it was. Come
on, I've got my car waiting. I'll take you back to the
hotel to get your things."

"No way." She drew back and took a deep breath.
"I'm not leaving."

"What do you mean you're not leaving?" He gazed
at her under narrowed eyebrows. "Just what are you
up to?"

"I want to know why that man didn't use the word
'proxy' in the marriage ceremony."

"It doesn't matter." He cursed under his breath and
reached for her arm. "Come on."

"It matters to me. Let me go and ask him."

Jon counted to ten. She might be beautiful, but she
was damn stubborn. How unlucky could one guy get?
he wondered as he gave in. "If it'll make you happy,
I'll go back and speak to Potter about it. You wait for
me." He urged her down the stairs and into his parked
car.

She was disturbingly lovely in a pink silk suit that
showed off her long, shapely legs and her well-formed
but slender body. A glimpse of a lacy slip didn't help
matters any. She was getting to him in ways he didn't
want to let himself contemplate. He took a longer,
speculative look before he reminded himself she was
a danger to his plans. It had been bad enough having

to marry Stacey, but at least she had felt the same way he did about matrimonial commitments. Their agreement to marry had a short time-line. But this woman—who knew what she was up to? "Here, get in and wait for me. I'll be back in a minute."

Jon called out to Potter and bounded up the steps of the Missoula, Montana, Courthouse to join him. "Sorry to keep you, Your Honor. But this marriage you just performed for me—it *was* a proxy marriage, wasn't it?"

"You're asking me?"

"Yes, well, I know it sounds strange, but the lady's a little nervous about the fact that you didn't include the word 'proxy' in the ceremony."

A frown crossed the elderly man's face. He stroked his beard. "Hmm. Married at least five couples today...say, yours was a strange wedding, wasn't it? That bride of yours almost changed her mind during the ceremony, didn't she?"

"Yes, but she did go though with it." Jon persisted. "It was a proxy marriage, wasn't it?"

"Never did see such a reluctant bride. Still, she is your wife."

"That's the whole point, Your Honor. Alexandra was just standing in for Stacey. Stacey Arden was the bride."

"You don't say? Things got a little confusing in there, you must admit." He eyed Jon for a brief moment before he continued. "Well, looks as if I might have married you to the wrong woman, doesn't it?"

Jon wasn't sure if Potter was putting him on, but just the thought of Alex Storm actually being his wife was more than he could handle right now. As far as he was concerned, he'd married Stacey as a matter of convenience. "You're not serious, are you?"

"Don't rightly know now, young man. I'll have to think on it. Check with me in the morning."

"Oh, hell!" Jon couldn't believe what he was hearing. It took all his willpower to keep from shouting at the judge.

"No use swearing, young man. The other marriages I performed today seemed to be in order. Maybe nothing is wrong, after all. Except my memory, of course. But since I seem to forget everything lately, it doesn't bother me anymore. Better check with the clerk over at the county courthouse tomorrow. They'll have the documents and you'll know the whole of it."

"This *is* the county courthouse, Your Honor."

"Then you don't have far to go to find out, do you?"

At the sight of Jon running his hands through his hair in a gesture of desperation, Alex shot out of the car and ran up the steps to join in the discussion. "Well, was it or was it not a proxy marriage?" she demanded. "I want to know right now."

Judge Potter sidestepped her wrath. "I can't help you, little lady. The clerk took all the papers to the records office right after your ceremony. Your husband will have to check the records tomorrow when they're recorded."

"He's not my husband, I was just—" Potter's words registered. "What do you mean? You just performed the ceremony a short time ago. How could you not know?"

The judge shook his mane of gray hair and backed away. "It's late in a busy day, and I'm not as young as I used to be. I don't know what difference waiting a day or two will make, anyhow." He slid away from Alex when she started to speak. As he left, he patted Jon on his shoulder. "You must lead an interesting life, young man. But I don't envy you one bit."

Alex closed her eyes and prayed. *Dear God, if you get me out of this mess, I'll never read the personal ads again.* She opened her eyes to face Jon. "Where does that leave us?"

"I'm not sure," Jon answered wearily. "I won't know until tomorrow."

"Tomorrow! I have to catch a plane tonight." Her eyes widened at the possibilities of a botched marriage ceremony. "What will we do if it turns out we're really married?" She shuddered and shook her head at his blank expression. "You don't look as if you really care. Do I need to remind you that you're supposed to be married to this Stacey Arden person and not to me?"

It was all Jon could do to concentrate on the trouble he was in without this spitfire distracting him. "I'm sure I'm married to Stacey. You're worrying for nothing."

Alex took a deep breath. "I suppose this isn't all your fault, but couldn't you find a justice of the peace with all his marbles?"

"Lord, deliver me," Jon muttered. He took Alex's arm and urged her into the car. "Get in. We can't settle anything this afternoon. The courthouse closed at five o'clock."

Alex yanked her seat belt in place. "Well, what are we going to do now?"

"Don't worry. Potter's a little forgetful. He's not the man he used to be. I'm sure he was just joking."

"Some joke. It's easy for you to say. I didn't come here to get married. All I wanted was a—"

"Story," he finished for her in an ominous tone. "No dice. I asked you to forget it!"

"Well, I can't! Proxy marriages are unusual, and a great story. I'm sure I can sell it."

"I don't want to have my private life laughed at over someone's breakfast table."

"Ever hear of freedom of the press?" Alex was gratified when he slowly nodded. "I can write anything I want to, especially since I'm the bride."

"I'm sure you're no bride of mine." He faced her coolly. "Not in a million years!"

"*Proxy* bride is what I meant to say."

"Proxy doesn't mean a damn thing—it's still not real. Try to remember that. But since you're so upset at the thought of being my wife, I'll check on it in the morning. Say, you're a free-lance journalist, right?" When she nodded, he continued. "Maybe no one but you is interested in proxy marriages," he said, more to reassure himself than her. "You got your money, so you can go." He wanted her to leave so he could go back to the hotel, call Stacey to tell her they were married and go on with his plans to become a father.

"Not until I'm sure I'm not your wife!" She pushed the money away and clamped her hands on her purse.

It was no use. The lady might be a spitfire, Jon admitted to himself, but if she was right, he couldn't remain angry with her. After all, if anything had gone wrong, it hadn't been her fault. Still, he'd watch himself, just the same. He put the bills away and mulled over his next move as he went around to the driver's side of the car.

Alex Storm was the first woman he'd found interesting in a long time, but he had the uneasy feeling she spelled trouble. He glanced at her as he examined the situation. He'd better keep his mind on the business at hand, he decided. If the lady was right, he already had more trouble on his hands than he wanted to contemplate.

He'd been drawn first by her appearance, but it hadn't taken him long to realize she had a quick wit that would be fun to spar with, and an independent spirit that made him want to try.

Maybe it was just as well she was leaving. The sooner, the better.

Alex watched the expression on his face gradually soften and an enigmatic smile briefly cross his face. She was dying to ask him what he was thinking about, but didn't want to get too far off the subject at hand. Not yet, not until she got the answer to her marital status and the story she came for.

She liked him, Lord knows why. Was attracted to him, actually. Maybe it was his green eyes sparkling in annoyance as they had a moment ago. Or his dynamite smile. Surely he hadn't really meant to try it on her, not when he'd just gotten married to someone else? Then there was his six-foot-plus muscular frame, his shoulders swinging purposefully as they'd left the courtroom. He never seemed to walk. He strode.

Everything about him was strong, determined. Well, so was she. She had a story to get, and she was going to get it.

"You know, Jon, from the way you've been acting, I'm beginning to think you're hiding something from me."

"That's absurd," he snapped. The smile disappeared and the guarded look was back.

"For a man with nothing to hide, you're awfully secretive."

"I like my privacy, that's all."

She preferred privacy for herself, too, in spite of trying to get a foothold in a profession that delved into secrets.

"I won't use your real name, if that's what's bothering you. I'm not interested in writing a story about you, for heaven's sake. It's the idea of a proxy marriage in this day and age that I find so interesting."

His silence continued as he glanced in the rearview mirror and stomped on the gas pedal. The car shot out from the curb into the lane of oncoming traffic. An angry motorist leaned on his car horn. Jon waved apologetically.

"Mr. Waring, that is, Jon...I can call you Jon, can't I?" At his nod, she asked, "Can we go someplace and talk?"

"What for?" His eyes narrowed as he glanced over at her.

"Just talk, that's all." A feeble request, she thought, in view of his desire for privacy.

"Only if you pick another topic of conversation."

"All right." Alex smiled innocently at him. She'd find another way to get her answers.

"How about dinner?" he asked after a thoughtful silence. "It's the least I can do after you flew out here from Chicago."

She knew they'd feed her dinner on the plane, but she wasn't going to turn down his invitation. After all, men as interesting as this one promised to be didn't come along every day.

Alex was more curious about him than ever. Why would a man like Jon Waring need to hire a proxy bride when no real woman could have resisted being by his side?

He looked to be in his mid-thirties, with a body that sent her hormones humming. He had unruly blond curls and a smile that was driving her to distraction. And tiny crinkle lines at the corners of his eyes—the mark of a man who smiled a lot. Not that he'd smiled much at her, but she couldn't blame him. Not when she'd almost left him standing at the altar, and, horror of horrors, confessed she was a would-be journalist.

And then there was that sensual aura about him. There was no doubt about it. He was quite a man, and the absent Stacey Arden a lucky woman.

Alex fought the sensuous, almost unmanageable, thoughts that came to mind every time she looked at her proxy husband, but it wasn't easy. She had no business thinking of him this way—the man was in love with someone else. And she had a plane to catch.

She considered the set look on his face. "You don't look too good. Aren't you feeling well?"

"That all depends on what you mean by 'well.'"

"A bridegroom is supposed to be happy."

"Only if he has his bride handy," he replied with a sardonic glance at her.

"Oh." Alex was subdued. "I hadn't thought about it quite that way."

"Think about it," he said dryly.

Alex thought about it. She blushed.

To hide her embarrassment, she whipped out her notebook and checked her notes. "Strange, isn't it, that Montana is the only state where proxy marriages are still legal?"

He hesitated before he answered her, trying to watch his step so she wouldn't get what she wanted. "I guess we Montanans like to be different. What got you so interested in proxy marriages?"

"I saw your ad in the newspaper and did a little research. By the time I was through, I was hooked."

She reached into her embroidered silk purse, took out the ad that had brought her to Missoula, Montana, and read, "'Wanted. Woman to stand in as proxy bride. Remuneration and expenses.'"

"It was news to me that proxy marriages were still legal in the United States. That's when I called you. I had the feeling that there are some great stories behind the custom. Yours seemed to have a lot of potential." When Jon threw a sharp look her way, she hastily added, "My interest is nothing personal, you understand. I honestly believe it's a subject readers would be interested in."

Jon silently considered his bad luck. Of all the possible women who could have read the ad, it had to be a would-be reporter who picked up on the offer.

Well, he thought, at least she wasn't an ordinary thrill seeker. Irrational women worried him; this one was intelligent enough to reason with, he hoped.

"Tell me again why you needed to get married by proxy. After all, it *is* unusual."

"I thought I told you on the telephone when we first talked. Stacey couldn't come home right now. She's in Paris on an assignment."

"And the marriage couldn't wait for her return?"

He stared at her impassively, not caring to guess at what was going through her mind. What did he expect? he wondered. A marriage so important that the groom couldn't wait for the bride to come home was enough to make any woman's imagination perk up. Especially someone like Alex Storm.

"It's no secret. The State Department's banned travel to and from the area Stacey is covering and she doesn't know when she'll be able to travel. Not only that, single women aren't welcomed in that part of the world. It's a lot easier for her to be a married woman."

"And you advertised in a Chicago newspaper for a proxy bride instead of here in Missoula?"

Jon grimaced. "I thought we were going to change the subject."

"In a minute. First, just answer this one question."

"All right, but remember, you've got only one answer coming. Understood?" When she nodded, he answered briefly. "For the same reason I don't want you to write about our marriage. For privacy."

Our marriage.

If it had been a real wedding with a groom of her own choosing, it would have been a different scenario. Her groom would have been someone she trusted and loved. Someone who wouldn't have dreamed of running out on her. She would have worn her mother's wedding dress and carried a bouquet of white and lavender lilacs. And when the wedding reception was over—

Alex's heart lurched at the images that came into her mind. A warmth started at her middle and shot its way upward until she felt her cheeks burn. She forced her thoughts to the wedding at hand and to remind herself she had been a proxy bride, nothing more. Stacey Arden was the bride. At least, she hoped it was Stacey and not her. Justice Potter's farewell remarks still worried her. Could Jon Waring actually be her husband?

Chapter Two

"I'm sorry," Jon offered as he pulled to a stop in front of Serrano's, a prominent restaurant in the older section of Missoula. "There's no need for me to be so edgy. If anyone's to blame for the wedding ceremony being botched, I guess it's Potter. We'll have to wait and see, won't we? Anyway, it's no way to treat a wife, is it?"

"I'm not your wife," Alex protested as she followed him into the restaurant. She subsided at the wry look on his face. He was right, they were better off parting amicably than in anger. "Oh well, but only for dinner. I have to catch a plane."

"Doesn't look as if I can hang on to either of my wives, does it?"

"How many wives do you have, for Pete's sake?" She gazed at him in wide-eyed amazement.

"Two, if you're right about the marriage ceremony." He cocked an eyebrow and grinned down at Alex.

"One," she answered firmly. "Stacey Arden."

"Right. I was just joking."

The maître d' materialized at their side. Alex saw him take in the corsage pinned to her festive suit, the flower in Jon's lapel and the shining new wedding band on her finger.

"An anniversary?"

"Wedding," Alex answered with a not-so-innocent smile at Jon. If he could make a joke out of this mess, so could she.

"Ah, yes. Definitely a wedding." A broad smile broke over the maître d's face. "I have the perfect table for your happy occasion."

He clapped his hands and murmured a quiet message to the waiter who had hurried to his side. Menus in hand, he led the way through a softly lit dining room to a corner table.

As the tuxedoed man seated Alex, she shot Jon a sardonic look. This was getting to be too much like a real wedding celebration. Especially when the maître d' lit the pink candles with a flourish.

"Ah, madam, the table was meant for you." He gestured to the candles and the soft mauve linens that complemented her pink suit. A moment later, he opened a bottle of chilled champagne the waiter had brought and filled their glasses.

"My congratulations, sir. And you, madam. May your future be a happy and fruitful one."

Alex stared after him in mock horror as he bowed and hurried away. She tried to repress the laughter that threatened to bubble forth like the bubbles in her glass of champagne.

Jon downed his drink. "What's so funny?"

"I feel more and more like a bride." She giggled as the bubbles hit the back of her nose.

"You find humor in that?" Jon's eyebrows rose in disbelief.

"It's better than crying."

"Over being a bride?"

"I guess so." Of course, she added silently, if ever she decided to try marriage again, a man like Jon Waring would be tempting. "All I wanted was some fun and a story. This whole bit is wasted on me. No offense," she hurried to add, "it has nothing to do with you."

"Thank goodness for that. I'd hate to think that being with me for a couple of hours soured you on marriage."

From the cynical way he'd replied, it was obvious to Alex that she wasn't the only one uncomfortable with the possibility they might be married to each other.

He seemed unusually preoccupied as he studied the menu. She'd have to turn on all her charm to get him to tell her why. Her woman's instincts clamored for the answer.

"Tell me something about yourself."

"What do you want to know?" he asked suspiciously from behind the menu.

"Ever been married before?"

"No."

"Well, if this is the first time, you certainly aren't acting overjoyed. In fact, I don't think I've ever seen a more unenthusiastic groom."

"Don't let it bother you," he finally replied as he lowered the menu and refilled his glass. Avoiding her eyes, he gazed around the nearly empty shadowed room. When he finally looked back at her, he wore a bland expression. For all the interest that showed on his face, she could have been talking about the weather.

Alex decided to switch tactics. There must be *some* way she could get the man to talk.

"After all, I did go through a wedding ceremony with you today," she protested. "That makes me sort of a wife. I'm supposed to care about you. I *did* promise Potter I would, and I never go back on a promise."

"'Sort of a wife'? That's a new one on me."

"For dinner, at least, remember?"

Jon gazed pensively at Alex. The tone in her voice had changed to something soft and warm. Up until now he'd had her pegged for an opportunist. This was a side of her he hadn't anticipated. Not that he thought she really cared about him, but he was willing to see how far she would go with this act.

She was enchanting in her attempt to lure him in and, as far as he was concerned, with her hazel eyes telegraphing an invitation at him, she sure had enough bait to make it interesting. Her appeal for him was more than just animal chemistry: she had a wit and intelligence that intrigued him. A soft smile curved at her lips and those hazel eyes shone with concern. He might have believed her, if he hadn't seen a glimmer of laughter lurking there. Well he knew from prior experience with Stacey that journalists would do anything for a story. He'd play the game for a while, but he was one fish she wasn't going to reel in. And one story she wasn't going to get. He just wanted to see how far she was prepared to go.

"I've always been an independent sort of guy." He smiled under raised eyebrows. "Actually, I hadn't thought much about getting married, until now. Too bad my wife is eight thousand miles away. Of course," he added suggestively, "if you're willing to break me in, I'm ready to put myself in your hands."

Alex blinked. Good Lord, she thought, how much of a bride did he think she was? She hadn't bargained on him being so ready to have someone other than his real bride to show him how to be a happy bridegroom.

"I...er...I didn't mean I wanted to show you how..." Her body warmed in embarrassment. Words failed her as she suddenly realized he was on to her. "Oh, never mind. I just thought you'd like to talk about what's bothering you."

"Right now, just you. How about it? Want to change your mind about breaking me in?"

Her eyes widened as his gaze teased over her. Mesmerized by the magnetic suggestion in his voice, she found it difficult to remember she was playing a game. She was so caught up by his personality and charm, she had to remind herself this wasn't a real wedding dinner and she wasn't a real bride.

She swallowed her chagrin. She should have known better than to try a wifely act on him. He was too intelligent to buy it. And furthermore, she thought with righteous indignation, he had no conscience, or he wouldn't be using his considerable charm to get even with her.

As for herself, it was troubling to think how much she enjoyed the idea of playing wife to a man she hardly knew and didn't know enough to trust. Even if the man was getting more and more interesting. She had to remind herself she wasn't ready to give up hope of a full-time newspaper career and she wasn't interested in falling for his invitation, either. Especially since a man she'd trusted before had made a fool of her.

Caution had to be the byword before she found herself in his arms, she reminded herself. There was no point in getting hurt again—for real or for fun.

"Just tell me, why did you have to hire someone to stand in for this Stacey of yours? Proxy marriages sound like pretty empty affairs."

Jon's eyebrows rose. "That's the second question. You only had one coming." He emptied his champagne glass while he gazed at the pert woman who was becoming more intriguing with each passing hour. She was no fool, but then, neither was he. Maybe, if he told her just enough, she'd leave him alone and go back to Chicago.

"I guess I can tell you that much—I'll never see you again." His gaze was firm as he prepared to tell her a half-truth. "But it's not for publication, understand?" He was prepared to tell his story when he saw Alex struggling with herself. No, he decided, he couldn't compromise himself just because her eyes gazed at him so expectantly.

He thought of young B.J. and the marriage he'd undertaken for her sake. He couldn't tell Alex the truth, not when B.J. and Stacey could be hurt.

Alex shifted uncomfortably in her seat under his contemplative stare and reached for a glass of ice water to cool her overheated body. "I promise I won't use your real names. Haven't you ever heard of the journalist's code of honor?"

She could tell he wasn't convinced when he glanced at her under raised eyebrows, that he believed she was a stubborn lady who thought she was too smart for him. He might be determined to keep his secret but she wasn't going to stop trying to get it out of him.

"No," Jon finally said, sitting back in his chair and eyeing her resolutely.

"Now see here, Mr. Waring. I went to a lot of trouble to come out here. You can't expect me to forget the whole thing." He was crazy if he expected her to bury a story that would make every reader sit up and take notice. She knew a dazzler when it came her way.

"And I paid you for your time and trouble." When she hesitated, he went on. "After all, that *was* one reason you took the job, wasn't it?"

"Yes, it was." Alex knew she was being foolish in refusing payment. What was the matter with her? She didn't have to apologize to anyone for needing the money. Five hundred dollars was more than she earned in two weeks. Earning it in two days was certainly an improvement.

"Well?" He held out the money. "Come on. You've earned it."

"And...?" she prompted as she accepted the bills.

"Drink up," he answered firmly. "Dinner is all you're going to get tonight."

"Want to bet?"

Jon leaned back in his chair and eyed her impassively. "Save your money. You'd lose."

The maître d' arrived to take their order and drew back at the looks on their faces.

"Something wrong, sir?"

"No, nothing," Jon said shortly as he studied the menu. He should have had his head examined before he invited her to dinner.

"Everything," Alex contradicted him.

"Perhaps dinner is in order, sir. May I suggest the chateaubriand for two?"

Jon nodded. "That would be fine. Alex?"

She shrugged.

The maître d' bowed and quietly departed for the kitchen.

"Not hungry?"

"No," she said, eyeing the basket of French rolls. Her stomach growled, but she was too fed up to care. "It isn't every day I run into someone as stubborn as you," she commented, "and it's not helping my appetite one bit. Anything I ate would probably taste like sawdust."

Jon's conscience stirred. This wasn't going to be a night to remember for either of them, but the least he could do was be polite. After all, it wasn't her fault that they were in this mess.

"Tell me something about yourself, Miss Storm."

She hesitated. Maybe, if they got on a better footing, he'd loosen up. "There's not much to tell. I studied journalism at the University of Illinois and I've been writing whenever I find time."

"Any luck?"

"Bits and pieces."

"I take it you don't have a steady job as a journalist," he said as he eyed her with interest. "What do you do for a living in between time?"

"Waitressing. Say," she said, catching herself, "you've got it all wrong. I'm supposed to be interviewing you!"

"Give it up, Miss Storm." His smile didn't reach his eyes. "Just pretend we're ships passing in the night. What time does your plane leave?"

Alex quit making patterns on the blush-colored tablecloth with her knife. "Around nine o'clock. Why?"

"The least I can do is to drive you back to the hotel and to the airport after dinner."

She was surprised at the offer. "I figured on taking a taxi. I thought you wanted to get rid of me as quickly as possible."

"Now, whatever gave you that idea?"

"I can't imagine what would have made me think so," she said, and laughed. She realized how ridiculous the whole scene was. "We seem to be getting along so well."

"Good. Then we can have dinner and enjoy it." He waved at the waiter, who stood at the kitchen door ready to wheel up the salad cart. "Let's get on with our wedding celebration."

Wedding celebration? Her heart skipped a beat, then raced to catch up. Determined to get what she came for, she tried one more time. "Come on, Mr. Waring. Sure you won't change your mind and tell me what's behind this marriage?"

"Eat your dinner. You think too much. Brides are supposed to let their husbands feel masterful. At least long enough to get through the wedding—"

"Wedding night?" Alex broke in and finished his sentence for him. When he raised his eyebrows and flashed a knowing look at her, she wanted to disappear under the table. Instead, she managed what she hoped was a sophisticated smile and dug into her salad. She breathed an inward sigh of relief when the waiter appeared to carve the entrée. Nine o'clock seemed an impossibly long time away.

"Tell me, just what it is you write, Alex Storm? Or is that your real name?"

"Alexandra, actually. But Alex looks better in print. I call my pieces "Stories from the Heart." She played with the medium-rare steak on her plate.

"If it isn't in the sports section, I haven't read it." Jon raised his empty glass to her. "Well, here's to your success."

At the kind gesture, all of Alex's journalist's instincts warred with her heart. But in the end, she couldn't help herself.

"Too bad your Stacey couldn't come home long enough to be married," she said.

When he quirked his eyebrows, she explained, "That's what I write about—the people in the stories. Their background. What made things happen, and why. I get a lot of ideas from personal ads. Like yours."

"Mine was that interesting?"

"Absolutely."

"Wrong again, Miss Storm," he answered, realizing he had to tell her something or she'd never let her questions rest. "Let's just say the reason for hiring a proxy bride concerns the welfare of a child very dear to me and leave it at that. You're off the hook. My own wife will be home soon."

When the waiter interrupted to pour coffee, Alex sighed with frustration. A child whose welfare concerned him? She was more curious than ever, but it sounded as if he had said all he was going to. She glanced at her watch. An hour or so more and she'd be gone. The sexy man across the table would take her to the airport and she'd never see him again. She sighed with relief—or was it with regret?

"Maybe we'd better get back to the hotel and pick up my luggage." She looked at Jon Waring, and knew just what the missing Stacey saw in him. His glance had an innate way of making a woman feel womanly, desirable. It was all there in his amused smile, the deep green eyes that seemed to be laughing at her now instead of sparkling in anger. He was the kind of guy she might have chosen in another lifetime.

Why were all the good ones taken?

And there was that certain mysterious aura about him that drew her. She felt its presence, responded to it in a way that made her heart race and her hormones fall over themselves. But he was married to someone else. No use asking for trouble.

"AH, MISS, ER..." The hotel manager on duty glanced down at the baggage receipt Alex handed him. "Ah, yes. Storm. I see you've made this visit a memorable one." He gestured to her corsage. "May I congratulate you both on your marriage. I hope you'll choose our hotel for your honeymoon. It won't take but a moment to open the bridal suite for you."

"The lady is leaving." Jon interjected firmly. "I need a room for myself. The bridal suite won't be necessary."

The manager did a double take. Alex tried to look nonchalant. It was a good thing no one could tell what she'd been thinking. The bridal suite had been on her mind for the past twenty minutes.

The more Alex thought about Jon and the way he affected her, the more she wished she knew more about him—and not only about his proxy marriage. From the way he looked and acted, he was obviously something more than a cowboy. There was a great story there, she was willing to bet on it.

Jon felt her thoughtful gaze on him as they waited for the bellhop to get her luggage. He gazed impatiently around him, praying he could get her to the airport before she started another round of questions. He was too late.

"So, what do you do when you're not getting yourself married?" she asked in a deceptively nonchalant voice.

He sighed and ran a hand through his hair. So much for trying to cut her off at the pass. He might as well give her some kind of an answer. What the hell, at least she wasn't asking about his reasons for the marriage.

"I'm the honorary mayor of Laurel, Montana, and president of its chamber of commerce."

"Laurel, Montana? What are you doing in Missoula?"

"Getting married, obviously."

"Why wouldn't you get married in Laurel?"

"I had my reasons."

"Really? Is that all you do?" Alex looked incredulous as she glanced at his wedding outfit. He didn't look her idea of a businessman, not in his Western getup, anyway. But maybe things were different in Montana.

"I own a ranch I inherited from my grandfather. I have a management company that helps run it. That leaves me time to do the things that really matter to me."

Yeah, sure, Alex thought. *The man must think I'm an idiot to buy that story. And that I'd be impressed with the hundred-dollar bill he left at the restaurant.* She decided to play along, for now.

"What's on the ranch. Cattle?"

"Among other things. To answer the question you asked me earlier, the company headquarters are in Chicago. That's why I advertised in the newspaper there."

"Do you come here to Missoula often?" She'd try once more, curious to see how long it would be before he tripped himself up again. Didn't he know that he was painting a picture of himself that was too good to be true?

"No, not anymore. I attended the University of Montana here in Missoula some years back." She saw him glance at her in wry amusement. Maybe he could tell she didn't believe a word he'd said. "Got any questions left?"

"Just one. What does your family think of this unusual marriage?"

"You're back to that, are you? Don't you ever give up?"

"It doesn't sound like a marriage made in heaven to me."

"Maybe not. How many marriages are?" He glanced at her, waiting for her to take the bait. She held her tongue. "What are you, a hopeless romantic?"

"For all the good it's done me, yes."

The cynical note in her voice got his attention. "You don't sound happy about wedding bells, either. Been married before?"

"No. And now that you mention it, I'm not married now, either."

"I didn't say you were." He held the hotel door open for her and waited for her to step outside to where his car was waiting.

Alex studied him out of the corner of her eye. When she'd first met him, he looked as though he were a simple cowboy. She was learning fast there might be a lot more to him than that. Too bad he was wasting it on an absentee wife.

Chapter Three

Carryon luggage stowed beneath the seat in front of her, Alex took her seat in the United 737 and gazed through the window. Night had fallen over the airport like a curtain. Halos ringed airport lights that glowed against the black velvet sky. A jitney truck hauling luggage snaked its way across the field. Catering trucks moved away from the plane. They would soon be leaving.

She thought about the past twenty-four hours and the odd proxy marriage she'd entered into. Every instinct she possessed told her there was something wrong with the ceremony, that the justice of the peace had somehow made a mistake. The more she thought about it the more she questioned the wisdom of leaving Jon Waring to take care of it.

Rummaging in her purse for a tissue, she glanced at the five folded one-hundred-dollar bills she'd been paid. She hoped it was only for being a proxy. She'd know soon enough, since Jon had promised to make sure. Well, she reassured herself as she gazed at the activity outside the plane's window, Jon Waring had been an honorable and decent man. He would do the right thing.

But not a man in love.

She thought back to their conversations about his marriage. If he and Stacey Arden had been lovers who decided to marry, he certainly hadn't acted like it. No, instinct told her he'd been far too evasive for her to believe it was the culmination of a love affair. He'd needed a bride for some other reason. A reason he had tried to keep secret.

Alex frowned as she recalled he'd said he was getting married for a child's sake. His and Stacey's child? Was Stacey pregnant? And, if the marriage was all that important to them, why hadn't Stacey somehow managed to come home for her wedding? Even if only for a few days? With a flash of insight, she knew her instincts had been right. Jon had been putting her on. There *was* a wow of a story there. She wasn't going to give up on it. Besides, she still wanted to know if she'd merely been a proxy bride or if she was really Mrs. Jon Waring.

She retrieved her bag from under the seat in front of her. Feeling like a salmon swimming upstream to spawn, she elbowed her way back to the first-class cabin door.

The stewardess looked surprised when Alex started through the plane's door.

"Sorry, but I have to get off."

The woman gave her a sympathetic smile. "What did you do, make a mistake?"

"Almost, but I think I caught it in time."

JON DROVE BACK to his hotel thinking about Alex Storm. To his surprise, he realized he'd actually enjoyed being with her, except for the ceremony, of course. Even in spite of the fact she'd wanted to know too much about his reasons for the proxy marriage. He had to give her credit; he could see she hadn't been satisfied, but she'd left for Chicago just the same. If only things had been different, he would have been sorry to see her leave.

He hadn't planned on getting married. Not until the court had told him he couldn't adopt young B.J. unless he had a wife. Not even when his best friends Bill and Nancy Saunders's will had designated him the guardian of their daughter in the event of their death. The caseworker had explained that a twelve-year-old girl needed a woman's understanding and advice at this critical time in her young life. And that there was a distant married cousin in New York who might be persuaded to take B.J.

Persuaded to take B.J. away from him? Hell would freeze over before he let that happen!

His heart ached for young Belinda Joan, or B.J., as almost everyone had called her since her birth. Losing her parents in a car accident had been so traumatic for her, for all of them. To allow the agency to place her with strangers in strange surroundings instead of with him would have been cruel. She was Montana born and bred and had lived in rural surroundings all her life. What would she do in a big city like New York? Not only that, she'd called him her uncle since she'd first learned to speak. He was the only security left in her young life. He'd left her home with a neighbor while he arranged to get married, but he intended to get back right away.

Not that he'd planned on becoming a father. The idea of raising a child and protecting her against the troublesome influences in society today gave him pause. But it was all the more reason to raise her on his ranch near a small town like Laurel. And as far as guiding her into becoming a young woman—the idea scared the hell out of him. As his parents' only child, the subject had never come up. And the only women he'd come across, except for Stacey, had been grown and knew the score. Maybe B.J. did need a woman's influence. For a time, anyway. But, first things first. He'd cross that bridge when he came to it. Right now, he had to get her a temporary mother.

He wasn't even sure he'd make a good father, but he intended to keep faith with his promise to Bill and Nancy. Even if it had meant marrying Stacey, a life-long good friend rather than a lover. Stacey was only doing him a favor by marrying him, to satisfy the court. Not that they intended to remain married for long. But revealing the truth to Alex Storm wouldn't have been fair to Stacey, or to B.J., either. He'd never do anything that would jeopardize B.J.'s adoption.

Jon thought with regret of the interest and compassion that had shone from Alex's expressive eyes. Eyes that blazed with fire when she was angry, glinted with flashes of gold when she laughed. He liked them both ways. Even her name suited her. Storm. She was quick, vibrant, full of energy. Challenging to be with.

His thoughts swung to Stacey, number one on the foreign correspondent's hit parade. On the surface, everything that had happened between them was almost as if it had been scripted by a screenwriter. Boy with a ready-made family marries the girl next door and they live happily ever after. If they only knew the truth!

Maybe he should have found an uncomplicated woman before now. One who would have been content to be a wife, a mother, to watch their children grow up together. Adopting and raising B.J. would have been a simple matter. But the truth was, he hadn't gotten around to being interested in marriage or fatherhood. Now, in a heartbreaking twist of fate, he'd gotten both.

"STACE? I'VE HAD A HELL of a time finding you! Are you okay?"

"I'm fine. How did everything go?"

"Right on schedule. We were married this afternoon. When are you coming home?"

He was surprised at the awkward silence at the other end of the phone. "Did you hear me? I said we're married."

"That's good, I guess. Now you can get the adoption started, right?"

"Right. You'd better come home as soon as you can." The hesitation in Stacey's voice finally registered. "Hey, what do you mean you guess so?"

"Well... I don't know how to tell you this, Jon, but things are really escalating over here. I can't talk about it over the phone, but I don't know when I can get back home."

"Say that again?"

"There's too much breaking news for me to leave now. You'll have to get by without me."

Jon was infuriated. "Come on, Stace. When you sent me the signed proxy marriage application, you said you'd only be gone a short time. Things have changed. I called home after the ceremony to check on B.J. Mrs. Llewellyn said the adoption agency had visited and was looking for me and my new wife. She told them we were on a short honeymoon to stall them, but that's only going to be good for a few days. You have to come home right away, or B.J. and I are going to be in deep trouble!"

"I'm sorry, but I told you I can't leave now, Jon. You'll just have to get along without me. Why don't you ask the proxy bride of yours to help you out?"

"I put her on a plane tonight. Besides, this isn't like asking someone to baby-sit B.J. for a few days. I can't ask a stranger to pretend to be my wife for goodness knows how long! And to top it off, she's a stranger who wants to know too damn much."

"I'm sorry, Jonnie. Really sorry. To tell you the truth, it's not only that I have a story to cover. It's more than that. I don't want to leave Faoud."

"Faoud? Who the hell is he?"

"Someone I met a few months ago," she said defensively. "We love each other."

"This guy Faoud can wait. B.J. can't. Come on, Stace. I need you back here. I can't lose B.J.!"

"I'm sorry, but Faoud and my job are just as important to me as B.J. is to you. I'm sure you'll be able to think of something until I get home. Got to yield the telephone. Take care!"

"Stace?" All Jon heard was a dial tone.

Swearing under his breath, he slammed down the receiver. Icy needles ran up and down his spine. He had to have a wife, preferably starting today and at least until Stacey was safely back in the United States. From the sound of it, that might be a long time. Maybe he could ask Alex to come back and pretend to be his wife. Just maybe she'd forget he hadn't been too friendly and do it for B.J.'s sake if he explained the situation to her. Only how would he explain the change in wives to the courts if Stacey didn't come home right away? For a guy who hadn't planned on marriage and fatherhood, he was knee-deep in both.

HE WAS MARRIED to Alex Storm and they were honeymooning on a sun-drenched Caribbean island. He was swimming after her in warm, pristine waters when she smiled back over her shoulder at him. It was a sexy smile, designed to send any man, let alone a bridegroom, out of his mind.

In a flash, he dived beneath her, caught her in his arms and pulled her under the water with him where he kissed her passionately. She returned his kiss and wound her legs around him.

Surfacing, he turned on his side and, with his wife in his arms, he swam to the warm, sandy shore. He drew the top of her bikini down over her breasts, kissing the glistening hollow beneath her throat. A moment more and the minuscule bikini was thrown onto the sand.

She held out her arms to him. When he reached for her, her fervent response almost pushed him over the edge. He moved to join their bodies and make her his at last.

"AH, MRS. WARING! Have you changed your mind and decided to remain with us tonight?"

"Well, yes. I'll need a room, please." It was easier to accept the title of Mrs. than try to explain. Besides, she'd waited at the airport until she was sure her "husband" was asleep, before returning to the hotel. She was tired and anxious to get some sleep so she could start her investigation in the morning.

"No problem," he said with a broad smile as he handed her a key.

Alex frowned. "This is Mr. Waring's room, isn't it?"

"Of course." The clerk gazed at her from under raised eyebrows as if to ask where else a bride would want to be.

Oh well, she thought as she smiled feebly and accepted the key. There were bound to be two beds in the room.

She was right. Jon was fast asleep in one, the blankets drawn over his head. Good, she thought as she undressed to her slip and slid into the other bed. She'd be up and gone before he awakened. He'd never know she'd been here.

Sleep wouldn't come. After a short time, she turned on her side, cradled her head in her arm and contemplated her sleeping "bridegroom." Her earlier wishful thoughts about a wedding night with this appealing man resurfaced. She warmed as she envisioned his arms around her, his lips on hers, his tongue seeking and finding her own. Somehow, her senses told her he would be a tender and yet fierce lover. And she would unleash all her pent-up longings for a man to love and to love her in return.

Her body ached for his touch as she finally drifted off to a troubled sleep.

SOMEWHERE IN THE distance, a telephone rang. He shook the sleep from his eyes and reached for the phone. He'd been dreaming, he realized with a flash of regret. A woman's insistent voice cut into his reverie.

"Jon Waring? It's Alex Storm. Remember me?"

Jon glanced around at the unfamiliar hotel suite as his body slowly cooled. There were no warm waters, no pristine sand. And the bride wasn't in his arms. She was on the telephone.

It took a moment to orient himself to the strange surroundings. What time was it, anyway? A quick look at his watch told him it was nine-thirty. Hell! He'd overslept when he should have been on his way home. And with damn good reason. It had taken him several hours to track down Stacey to tell her they were married. When he'd heard what she had to say, he'd had to fight off the impulse to grab a plane to Paris to throttle her and drag her back home. Instead, he'd taken several healthy swigs of brandy and fallen asleep.

Only he obviously hadn't slept too well.

"Yes," he mumbled while he tried to pull himself together. How could he forget his proxy "bride"? Those tempting eyes set in a porcelain pixie face had continued to haunt him from the time he'd waved goodbye at the airport. Her musical laugh when she'd insinuated he was a fraud had echoed in his sleep. Her determined nature and single-mindedness had intrigued him even when his common sense had told him to forget her. He hadn't been sure if he'd wanted to kill her or kiss her, but there'd been something intriguing about her that had made him want to do further research. No wonder he'd dreamed of honeymooning with her.

Except, of course, he *was* married to someone else. Wasn't he?

He remembered Alex Storm, all right. Now, all he had to do was to persuade her to come back to Laurel with him and to pretend she was his wife for as long as it took for the adoption agency to set eyes on her. And to promise never to tell anyone the truth. And then, in self-defense, he'd pay her off and send her home, never to see her again. Only, how could he control his dreams?

"Sure," he said, his mind racing with possibilities. "How was your flight? Did you get home all right?"

"Actually, I'm downstairs."

"You're where?" His heartbeat quickened as he came wide-awake. Alex Storm was in the hotel. Thank God for miracles. "Here in Missoula? I put you on a plane for Chicago last night."

"I deplaned and came back to register in the hotel." He heard a laugh in her voice.

"What's so funny?" he asked, holding his aching forehead. The throbbing that almost blinded him did nothing for his peace of mind.

How could she tell him the truth about her staying in his room last night? And the irony of her reaction to him lying in the bed only inches away from her?

"I needed to talk to you."

"Talk, that's all?" He didn't believe her for a minute, not when the hairs on the back of his neck were vibrating warning signals like crazy. There was trouble waiting for him, but at least she was here when he needed her. "Good. I have to talk to you, too."

"Okay, but first I'm going to the county courthouse to check the records. I want to know what kind of marriage we entered into. There are too many unanswered questions in my mind to suit me."

It was all Jon could do to keep from groaning. Alex's resolute voice wasn't doing much for his brandy hangover, but the fact remained, he had to talk to her. Maybe they could compromise.

"Stay in the lobby. Don't step out of the door without me. I'll dress and be down right away." He threw off the covers as he spoke and headed for a quick, cold shower to clear his head.

HE FOUND HER BROWSING in front of the hotel boutique window. Just like a woman, he growled under his breath. Even in a crisis, shopping was the first priority. When he called to her, she spun around and waved at him. Her look of determination belied her previously stated intention to go home and let him take care of their possibly botched marriage ceremony. Lord, that's all he needed—a tenacious woman. No wonder she'd lied about going home. If she was that upset over a proxy ceremony, what would she say to acting out the marriage for the benefit of the courts? A studied smile on his face, he strode toward her.

Alex stood her ground and held out her hand. "Before you say anything we may both regret, remember we're in this together. I hope we can be friends."

Friends. Sure. After his conversation with Stacey, he'd planned more than friendship with Alex Storm.

"What makes you think we can't be friends?" He let go of her hand and gazed at her.

She cleared her throat and tried a hesitant smile on him. "That sounds like a threat. I hope I'm wrong. What will it be, friends or . . . ?"

"Friends." Her winning smile was getting to him in spite of his resolve not to be too involved with the lady. He would have to be careful. If he were an honorable man, he'd tell her what he had in mind right now. Tell her that he wanted to take her home to meet the adoption agency worker, to pretend to be his wife. Except that it would give her the story she was looking for. He raked his hand through his hair. What a mess.

He bestowed a noncommittal smile on her. "Okay, friends, Alexandra."

"My friends call me Alex," she answered nervously. Now that he was making an effort to be charming, she hardly knew what she was saying. It was the Western way he drawled her name that made her cheeks flush and her hands tremble. Each drawn-out syllable of her name had a soft, suggestive sound. An invitation.

"Is it all right for this friend to call you Alexandra? It suits you."

"Yes, of course." Alex swallowed her nervousness, cleared her throat and forced a smile. "Now that we're friends, I have a favor to ask."

"What did you have in mind?" He rubbed the back of his neck.

"I want to go over to the courthouse."

He changed his mind about asking her to go home with him right away. Hopefully, the papers were wrong, and, if all went well, he'd ask her then.

But what if she were right? That they were man and wife? Heaven forbid. Asking her to come home with him might be impossible then. He had no doubt she'd be too angry to appeal to or to reason with. He'd have to stall for time, to think of ways to present his proposition reasonably.

Alex got right down to business.

"That Justice Potter who married us. I can't help feeling there's something wrong with the ceremony he performed."

Her expression dared him to contradict her and he was tired of trying. Still, he had to cut her off at the pass. "Why? I told you Potter's mind is one card short of a full deck, but he's harmless. He actually retired five years ago, but the regular justice of the peace got married recently and went off on a prolonged honeymoon. Potter came in to perform marriage ceremonies as a favor to District Judge Simmons."

"That's nice for Judge Simmons, but not for me. It's a good thing weddings are all Potter does," she said darkly. "If he was asked to conduct criminal trials, he'd probably hang the wrong man."

He groaned his despair. "Alexandra, your imagination is running away with you."

"All I want to know is, did Potter know the difference between a proxy marriage and a real one?"

"You can't actually believe we're legally married?"

"Well, maybe not exactly a real marriage. But something is definitely wrong, I can feel it in my bones. If I'm right, this mess isn't going to be easy to untangle. Besides, I'm not interested in being married," she answered. "It would be inconvenient."

Inconvenient, she'd said. If she only knew. Wait until she found out what he had in mind for her.

He took a deep breath and counted to ten. Maybe it *was* time to find out who he was legally married to. Not that it really made any difference in the long run, he realized with a sigh. He needed Alex Storm and he needed her silence. Maybe being married to her *was* the answer. "It doesn't make a difference if Potter left a word out of the ceremony. It's the papers we signed that count."

"You didn't give me a chance to read them," she retorted. "Remember the way you rushed me from the courtroom? We were both too anxious to get out of there to stop to read the documents before we signed them, remember?"

"Yes, well . . ." What could he say? It was true. For that matter, he hadn't taken the time to read the papers himself. After the unexpected way his proxy bride was acting, he hadn't been able to get out of the courtroom fast enough.

"Some husband material you are. You're not even interested in finding out who you're married to." She gathered her purse and a small briefcase. "I'm ready for the lion's den, are you?" When he still hesitated, she chided, "If you're really not afraid of what we might find, can we please go over to the courthouse now? I'd like to catch Potter when he's wide-awake."

ALEX FOUND JUSTICE OF THE Peace Homer Potter on his hands and knees searching the floor of the courtroom. Jon's echoing footsteps as he followed behind her sounded like thunder on the polished wooden floor. Empty wooden spectator pews smelled of oil polish and wax. Dim light filtered through the stained glass windows into the quiet room. Whatever Potter was looking for wasn't going to be easy to find.

A stop at the courthouse records office was premature. Her only hope of getting an answer lay with Potter, Heaven help her.

There was a burning taste at the back of her throat as she tried to swallow her anxiety. The tiered jury box was intimidating. She was only here to interview Potter. Why did she feel her life was on trial?

Homer Potter looked up when she and Jon came into the courtroom. He heaved a sigh of relief. "Good. I can use a little help. Come in, come in, don't just stand there."

"Help? Help with what, Your Honor?" Afraid it might be a contact lens Potter was looking for, Alex stepped gingerly over to Potter's side with Jon carefully following in her footsteps.

"Lost my hearing aid. The dratted thing dropped out of my hands when I was getting ready to put it in my ear. Don't really need it, you understand. Only when I'm officiating at a marriage." His voice was muffled as he bent to search around him. His nose almost scraped the floor.

"Sure thing, Your Honor." Alex dropped to her knees and joined in the search. No wonder Potter couldn't remember the details of yesterday's ceremony. He probably hadn't heard any of it.

It took only a moment for her to find the hearing aid under the courtroom stenographer's machine where it had rolled. She retrieved it and handed it to Justice Potter.

"Thank you." Potter inserted the device, then tested its volume by intoning, "How now, brown cow?" He made an adjustment and looked inquiringly at Alex. "Now, what can I do for you folks?"

Alex felt like the Alice who had gone through the looking glass and into Wonderland. This was a presiding justice of the peace?

She took a deep breath and plunged right in.

"Perform many proxy marriages, Your Honor?"

"Oh, no. Not nowadays." Potter rose to his feet and dusted off his knees. "I'm actually retired, you know."

"A few?" Alex persisted.

"Not that I can recall."

Jon held up a warning hand when Alex clenched her fists.

"One or two?" she asked.

"Could be." Potter pulled up a chair and smiled at his audience. "Now, it was a whole different story a hundred years ago when men were afraid to leave their holdings long enough to go back East to get a bride and bring her back here. Outlaws, you know?''

Alex nodded her encouragement and sat down to listen. Now that Potter was on the subject of proxy marriages, surely he would remember hers.

Maybe proxy marriages had worked out fine a hundred years ago, but his own wasn't doing so well, Jon thought sourly. Until he saw the delighted smile on Alexandra's face. Maybe she was more human than he'd given her credit for. Maybe it wouldn't be too hard to convince her to go home with him.

"Yes, sir, just fine. Too bad life got so complicated." Potter sighed over happier times and opened his eyes to peer at Jon. "Got yourself married here recently, didn't you, son?'' His gaze swiveled to Alexandra. "Mighty pretty young lady, if I may say so.''

Jon was relieved to hear Homer Potter could still appreciate a pretty woman. Maybe his befuddled manner was just an act.

"This is Alexandra Storm, Your Honor. She stood in as proxy for my fiancée, Stacey Arden. Stacey couldn't make it back from Paris for the wedding.''

The judge peered at him. "I remember now. You'd think the other bride could have managed to come home to marry you herself. Maybe you're better off with this one.''

Jon heard Alex gasp in the background. With Potter acting as though she were available for the taking, Jon couldn't blame her for reacting. Especially when Potter had gone far enough to suggest that Jon make the choice between her and Stacey.

Potter dismissed the sound and continued. "I seem to recollect you were going to look at the record to make sure you were married to the right woman."

"We're on our way right now."

"Well, good luck." The elderly man yawned and looked around the empty courtroom. "No one's interested in getting married, I see. Guess I might as well go home and take a quick nap before lunch."

He might have been joking, but Alex was alarmed at the flippant comment. The time had come to settle this mess, and she was ready to do it. She moved past Jon and stood almost nose to nose with the startled justice. "Your Honor, ours *was* a proxy wedding, wasn't it?"

Potter gestured vaguely.

Jon shrugged helplessly.

Alex made for the door, muttering under her breath, "This isn't happening." Whirling, she turned on Jon. "Are you coming, or not?" He couldn't meet her eyes.

Before he had a chance to move, the document clerk burst into the courtroom. Waving a piece of paper, she blurted, "I've got it!"

Alex jumped forward and snatched the document from her hands. She could feel Jon breathing down her neck as she studied the marriage certificate. Potter had inserted Alex's name as the bride on the marriage certificate and he had signed his name to the certificate.

For all intents and purposes, she and Jon Waring were legally married.

Chapter Four

"What do you have to say about this mess?" Alex couldn't stop fidgeting in the vinyl booth of a nearby coffee shop.

A wry smile came over Jon's face as he slid into the opposite seat. "Will 'I'm sorry' do?"

"Sorry!" She looked deeply affronted. "Sorry doesn't begin to cover it!"

"You're right. I'm as shocked as you are," he said. "After all, I'm married, too, you know."

"Well, you wanted to be married," Alex retorted.

Jon could tell she wasn't satisfied. He didn't really feel sorry or shocked, either, for that matter. Now, he could get down to the big question.

"This has to be one of the dumbest things I've ever heard of." She was sputtering, she was so mad.

Jon watched her, amused that she could be so angry and still remain attractive at the same time.

But back to business. He'd reached the point of no return. Hoping that she couldn't possibly get any angrier, he popped the question.

"How would you like to make another five hundred dollars?"

He was stunned by the range of emotions that played across her face. Shock turned into disbelief, disbelief into suspicion and finally anger. Not that he blamed her. He'd approached the subject like a tornado roaring across Kansas, but then, subtlety wasn't his style. He believed in cutting to the chase. Maybe he should have taken his time, approached her later. But time wasn't what he had.

"We've just found out we've been married to each other by mistake and you want to know if I'd like to make another five hundred dollars? You must be out of your mind!"

Jon was taken aback by the change that came over her. Her eyes blazed fury, all five feet two inches of her telegraphed her indignation. Even her clenched fists spoke of her frustration. He had to do something, and fast, before she suited physical action to words. And, from the expression on her face, it was beginning to look as if she were capable of it.

"If you give me a few minutes, I'll explain. As a matter of fact, this may turn out to be beneficial for both of us."

Alex muttered something under her breath but sat back to listen.

"Since we're in this together we're going to make the best of things. As for the five hundred dollars, I didn't mean to insult you. I'm prepared to tell you the whole truth and nothing but the truth." He held up his right hand. "So help me God."

"Tell me now," she said, looking as if she weren't prepared to trust him further than she had to.

"The truth is, I need a real wife for a while."

"What's wrong with waiting for your Stacey?"

"A lot. That's the problem. Fortunately, or unfortunately, depending on the way you look at it, Mrs. Waring, I need you."

Jon downed the remainder of his coffee and turned his attention to Alex. His wife? Even the district judge, who certainly should have known procedure hadn't had a ready answer for him. It seemed that intent might have had something to do with the case, but the botched marriage had clearly set a legal precedent.

The judge had been temporarily at a loss to give advice. Outside of an annulment, he'd finally announced, after much judicial pondering, Jon was married to Alex. And, heaven help him, Jon reflected, an immediate annulment was out of the question. He needed her until B.J.'s adoption went through.

He frowned at the idea of Alex Storm as his wife. She was bent on a career as a writer, he was a man of the soil. She lived in a big city, he lived in a log cabin outside a small town of seven thousand souls.

There wasn't a thing they had in common.

He stole a glance at her pink silk suit, manicured fingernails and soft, white skin that spoke of spending her days and nights indoors. Outside of pretending to be B.J.'s mother, what good would she be on a ranch?

None of that mattered now. He had to have a wife, and like it or not, Alex Storm was it. Without one, the courts appeared to be determined to place B.J. with a distant cousin. In New York City, of all places! B.J. was as frisky as a colt and just as irrepressible. She'd be stifled in the rigid confines of a city apartment. She needed open spaces as much as he did.

"What I'm about to tell you is in the strictest confidence," he said softly after glancing around to make certain no one was near. "And that means *no one* else must ever know about it. It's just between the two of us."

Impressed in spite of herself by the serious tone in his voice, Alex nodded her agreement.

"What this all amounts to is that I need a wife in order to become a father."

"You want to become a father?" Alex, her eyes widened in horror, echoed in a whisper. "And you decided to choose your child's mother through a want ad? Of all the dumb..."

"Hold on a minute. It's not as bad as it sounds."

"No, indeed. It's worse!" She grabbed her purse and started to slide out of the booth. "I don't want any part of you and your crazy ideas!"

His hand shot out and grabbed her wrist before she had a chance to make her getaway. "At least, let me explain."

"You've explained enough." Alex tried to loosen his firm grip on her hand. "I'm getting tired of your manhandling me. Any more of this and I'm going to call the police. Personally, I'm beginning to believe I was right. You *are* out of your mind!"

He wouldn't let go. "Sit still, damn it, you're beginning to attract attention," he said with a tight smile that didn't reach his eyes. "At least give me a chance to tell you the whole story."

When she reluctantly nodded, he released her hand. "I'll give you ten minutes," she warned, ready to make a run for it, "and then I'm out of here."

"Okay, okay!" He went on to tell about Bill and Nancy's deaths and B.J. "Anyway, their will designated me as her guardian."

"Oh, so that's the baby you mentioned earlier!" Alex was pleased with herself. Her instincts about why Jon Waring needed to get married had been right on target.

"What baby?" He looked at her blankly. "B.J.'s almost twelve years old!"

"Sorry." Alex blinked. Things were moving too fast for her to keep up. "Frankly, I thought you were trying to tell me you and Stacey were expecting a child and that was the reason for the marriage."

He looked at her as if she were the one who'd lost her mind. "Hardly. Anyway, as I was saying, I was asked to be B.J.'s guardian in the will."

"And?"

"The courts evidently don't agree."

"Why not? It may be a little unusual for a single man to adopt a child, but surely parents have the right to choose a guardian for their children."

Privately, in his case at least, she wasn't so sure the courts weren't dead right.

"You would think so," he replied with a scowl. "But some fool social servant decided that B.J. is turning twelve and needs the comfort and advice of a woman. She's only a kid, for heaven's sakes!''

Alex reached for her coffee cup. Jon Waring's story began to make sense, and, she thought with an inner pang, was beginning to sound familiar. ''Take it from me, a twelve-year-old girl is on the threshold of adolescence. She needs to be made comfortable with the idea.'' She smiled in sympathy at the flush that came over his face. ''It sounds to me as if they're absolutely right. And that's where Stacey fits in?''

''Yeah, except Stacey couldn't stick around long enough to get the job done.''

''So you decided on a proxy bride?''

''Yes. But, so help me, I never expected it to turn out this way.''

Alex gazed into his earnest green eyes. What it came down to, was no matter how she and Jon Waring felt about each other, he needed her. And so did a little girl named B.J. The story brought an ache to her heart. Whatever she thought of the situation had to take second place.

Strangely enough, she'd felt an inner need to help him from the first time she'd noticed the unhappy look in his eyes. And now she realized why. She was almost ready to agree. Until she heard Jon say it would be a temporary arrangement until Stacey came home. Alex would be free to go back to Chicago. And, when the need for a wife was over, even Stacey intended to leave.

The pragmatic way he described his plan bothered her. She had herself to consider, too. Who would care about the way she might feel when the time came for her to leave? she wondered. She hesitated before saying yes. One broken heart was enough to last her a lifetime.

"It will be only for a few days, or until Stacey finishes her assignment," Jon explained. "I hate to put you out, but I really care about B.J."

"I'm not sure about this," she answered slowly. "Actually, I'm not sure I want to be married, even for a short time."

"I know how you feel, I felt the same way, too," he said, mistaking her hesitancy for a reluctance to being tied down to responsibility. "Fact of the matter is that I had no intention of getting married, either." He gave a short laugh. "As far as I can see, marriage ties you down. You wind up caring too much, doing too much to think about your own plans. Yep, I confess I enjoy my freedom. But I'd do anything for B.J. I've loved the kid since she was born."

Alex valued her freedom, too, but it was at odds with her nurturing nature and her own need to love and cherish someone who would love and cherish her in return. "I'll be honest with you, too," she confessed. "I've been in one relationship that ended badly, and I'm not crazy about being hurt again. And, after all, a proxy marriage is one thing, but a stand-in wife for weeks is something else."

"It won't take weeks," he assured her. "I'm sure Stacey will see the light and come home."

"How can you be so certain?"

"You'll have to trust me." As if aware something deeper than the proxy marriage was bothering her, he went on. "You don't have someone waiting for you at home, someone you care for, do you?"

Alex wished the proxy marriage had never taken place. Her senses were telling her how much she wanted to go with this man, even as her common sense was telling her to go slowly, if at all. She might be setting herself up for another fall if she got involved with him. One Tim in her life was more than enough.

"No," she said quietly as she looked down at her clenched hands. "I don't have someone waiting for me."

"Then tell me what you're afraid of? If it's me, I promise to respect you and your wishes. It's not for me, it's for B.J. Please think about it."

As he spoke, she realized Jon wasn't offering himself. A child needed her. So what was she so afraid of?

"Maybe this will help make up your mind." He took his wallet from an inner pocket in his jacket and withdrew a snapshot. "This is a recent picture of B.J. It was taken when she and her folks visited my ranch during Easter vacation. She's a sweetheart, isn't she?"

Alex took the snapshot he handed her. In it, a lovely young girl was laughing into the camera. Wind had whipped her brown hair away from a pixie face, revealing the maturing features of a girl that almost matched Alex's own. With a feeling of déjà vu, she realized B.J. resembled herself as a twelve-year-old.

"Do you love Stacey, or was it going to be a marriage of convenience?" she asked.

"I care for Stacey very much. As a matter of fact, we were engaged in college. But, no, she's just doing me a favor."

"How far would this marriage of ours go?" she finally asked, after pulling herself together. She was embarrassed to meet his gaze, and hoped the blush she felt come over her wasn't obvious.

"Only as far as pretending to be a mother to B.J. You have my word on it." Jon gazed thoughtfully at Alex, saw her discomfiture and the blush that swept her face. She'd quieted down now that he'd assured her their marriage was to be temporary, and platonic.

"Well then, if you're sure I fit the bill, I'll go along with you and pretend to be your wife." She needed the money and she hadn't given up on the story. She saw a lifted eyebrow and surprised smile come over his face.

"You will? After all that's happened, frankly, I'm relieved. From the way you were taking our marriage, I expected more of an argument."

"Yes. Normally I would." Alex's gaze locked with his. "But I have my reasons. I want to make it clear I intend to be just passing through. No involvement... no strings."

"Care to explain the reasons?" He was moved by the vulnerable look that came into her eyes.

"It's no secret. I can't afford to become deeply involved, it would be too difficult for me to leave later." She hesitated, took a deep breath and went on. "As a matter of fact, I was adopted when I was a little girl about B.J.'s age. Until then, I was raised in a series of foster homes. I know how much it would mean to B.J. to have a stable environment and to have you for a father. That's the only reason I'm prepared to go with you."

The simple truth was, although she'd never met the child, she already cared about what would happen to B.J. The real problem facing her was she was beginning to care for Jon, too. The anguish in his eyes when he'd told her B.J.'s story, the relief that came across his face when she'd agreed, told her a great deal about the man. He was more human than he'd been willing to admit. What she'd thought was pure stubbornness at not revealing the truth behind the proxy marriage had been loyalty and the desire to protect a helpless young girl.

It took a real man to want to raise someone else's child.

Of course she could play mother to B.J. As for Jon Waring, he wasn't hers to consider. She tried to ignore the butterflies fluttering in her stomach. And the hormones that stood at attention at the thought of playing Jon's wife.

"You'll have to think of a believable story about how we met and where I've been all this time," she reminded him. "We *are* strangers, after all."

Jon signaled for a refill of their coffee cups. "Not for long, I guess. Not if we want to make this look realistic. As for a story, I figured I could leave that up to you. That's your area of expertise, isn't it?"

"That's easy," she said after a moment's reflection. "Didn't you say your corporate headquarters are in Chicago? We can always say we met there."

"Right." Jon came to life. The first hurdle was over. "We can say we met when I traveled East on business, if anyone asks." He took a deep breath of relief. "But remember, the truth of our marriage status has to be just between you and me. Not even B.J. is to know."

"I'm not sure that's wise. Children are hard to fool. What will she think when Stacey shows up and I have to leave?"

"B.J. knows I came here to get married by proxy to Stacey. Later, I'll get around to explaining that Stacey couldn't make it back. For now, that's all she needs to know. As for what comes later, I don't even want to think about it. Hopefully, the adoption agency will be out of the picture by that time."

Jon drained his cup and glanced around for the waitress. The thought of inevitably losing Alex wasn't something he wanted to think about. She had an air about her that intrigued him. An independence that challenged him. And a heart bigger than he had been giving her credit for.

No, he thought as he paid the bill and waited for Alex to join him, there'd never been another woman who'd made such a deep impression on him so fast, and, in spite of the fact that there were a dozen reasons they were so thoroughly incompatible, never one he was so reluctant to let go.

Chapter Five

Calico foothills hung low against the horizon. The setting sun cast its glow over endless vistas of waving prairie grass. The rolling landscape was quiet and empty; they were miles from nowhere. For a woman used to the busy streets of Chicago, the silence that surrounded her was eerie, the rolling sea of grass intimidating.

Alex took a shaky breath, stirred uneasily and called herself all kinds of a fool. What was she doing, putting her trust in a man she'd met only two days ago? It had been more than the money and the possibility of a story that had decided her. It was Jon's wanting to adopt a child that had brought her here, but now that they had almost reached their destination, she was beginning to doubt her sanity.

He turned off the highway and stopped at a rustic gate and cattle guard. The weathered sign claimed the hard-packed dirt road they were entering the property of the Blue Sky Ranch. Jon reached over her to the glove compartment for a remote control, a modern device that seemed at odds with the aged wire fence. With a press of his fingers, the gate swung open.

"All this belongs to you?" Alex's skepticism about what Jon had told her about himself vanished in a sea of guilt when he nodded. But not the undercurrent of anxiety she still felt about the wisdom of agreeing to go to such a remote place.

"It must be awfully lonesome out here," she murmured as she gazed around her.

"Not at all," he answered cheerfully. "Nature makes good company. Besides, it's a lot healthier living out here than in a big city."

Out of the corner of her eye, she could see his amused smile, the calculating glance he threw her as he started the motor.

"You look surprised," he said. "Didn't believe me when I told you about myself and the ranch, did you?"

"No," she said defensively. Although what she had to be defensive about was beyond her. It had been all his fault, throwing around half-truths and hundred-dollar bills as if to impress her. And leaving her to worry about her decision to go with him. "I didn't know what to think. You were so secretive back there, I thought you were putting me on."

From his raised eyebrows, there was no doubt in her mind that he'd known all along she didn't believe him for a minute, but he *had* sounded too good to be true. She felt like a fool. What else was she going to find out about him?

He must have sensed her mixed emotions, for he started to tell her more about himself in a matter-of-fact tone that was more calming than the details he provided.

"My great-grandfather homesteaded here over one hundred and fifty years ago. With the exception of some modern-day improvements, the land is pretty much now as it was then. Outside of a small place in Laurel where my Dad practiced medicine and stayed overnight occasionally, my family has lived here ever since."

"Are there many of you?" Alex belatedly realized Jon could have persuaded some female member of his family to take responsibility for B.J. Why hadn't he?

"Unfortunately, there's only Mom and Dad and me. They've been doing a lot of traveling now that Dad's retired. In fact, they're somewhere in Europe right now. I have a few distant cousins on Dad's side scattered around the country, but they have families of their own. Too bad, too. Granddad always envisioned dozens of his descendants enjoying the ranch."

He sounded the car horn and waved at two distant horsemen galloping by. "I guess we've never been a prolific family. We sure could use a few kids around the ranch. Thank goodness for B.J. She took to living on the place like a duck takes to water. The little squirt can ride the range and rope a steer with the best of them," he said proudly.

"Maybe that's the trouble," Alex sniffed.

"Trouble? What do you mean by that?"

"B.J. is a girl, even if you have her behaving like a tomboy. You keep talking about her as if she's actually a boy."

Jon looked surprised. "No, just a kid. But I guess that's why the social service people figure I need you. Still," he insisted, "I like her just as she is."

"And what does B.J. want?"

"I haven't heard any complaints yet," he muttered under his breath. He headed toward a series of low, weathered structures. "Just remember, this whole thing between us is only temporary."

"Of course," she answered quietly, hoping that "temporary" would be short and not too draining. "Is that your home over there?"

"No. We still have a mile to go before we reach the ranch house. Blue Sky is one of the largest holdings around here," he commented as they drove past the buildings. "Those are storage sheds. When winter sets in and the grass is buried under snow, we feed the stock from hay we store in there.

"By the way," he added, gesturing to her pink silk wedding ensemble. "Tomorrow, we'll have to drive into Laurel and get you some clothes more suitable for ranch life. That outfit is mighty impressive for weddings, but it won't do for cooking and cleaning."

At that she bridled. "First of all, I didn't intend so stay more than one night so I only brought this suit. And a few . . . never mind," she added when his eyes raked her outfit. "Secondly, if you wanted someone to cook and clean, you should have hired yourself a housekeeper. I'm not it!" Annoyed by his attitude, she forgot the landscape and turned her attention to his comments. "Besides, you advertised for a proxy bride. What did you expect me to look like if not a bride?

And, you never told me I was to do anything more than pretend I was a stepmother to B.J.!''

"I expected you to play the whole nine yards of the role. But since you brought it up, I already have a part-time housekeeper who comes in twice a week. And there's Cookie, who feeds the ranch hands and who dishes up darn good meals when she's not around. But, as I recall," he said as he cast another amused glance at her outfit, "when I was growing up, my mother was happy to keep up the house and was the best cook in the county!"

Alex ignored the facetious remark. He was right. Mothers did cook and clean, as well as nurture. Hers certainly had. And a lot more, besides. She glanced down at the pink moire pumps that matched her silk suit. What had possessed her to buy an outfit a real bride might choose for her wedding? Especially since she'd sworn off marriage altogether? Maybe it was the romantic streak in her. Maybe, she *had* wanted to feel like a bride or she wouldn't have been thinking about honeymoons. Whatever had prompted her to spend some of her hard-earned savings, she could have saved herself the trouble.

She felt like a fish stranded on dry land.

"By the way, I'll have to get to a phone and call the restaurant. They expected me back for the weekend."

"You can call from the ranch house," he chided. "Even out here in God's country we've joined the twentieth century. You'll find we have all the modern conveniences you might want. And," he added as he glanced pointedly at her stylish wedding outfit, "from the looks of things, you'll want to avail yourself of all of them."

He watched her features stiffen. Damn! He'd put his foot in his mouth again. If he kept this up, he'd never get her cooperation, let alone convince anyone they were newlyweds. Newlyweds were supposed to have stars in their eyes. His bride's eyes spoke volumes, and they weren't exactly telling love stories.

"I'm sorry," he apologized, patting her hand where it lay on her silk skirt. "I don't suppose that's any way to treat a wife, is it?"

He was surprised to find her hand cold to his touch, an indication of her inner unrest. He had no right to make remarks about her and her Eastern life-style, let alone how she dressed. Or to sit in judgment. Not everyone was lucky enough to have been born and bred to enjoy the earth and nature's bounty, as he had been. Stricken by remorse, he squeezed her hand. "Truce?"

"Just keep in mind that I'm not your wife, Jon Waring," she retorted as she reclaimed her hand and straightened out her skirt. "And try to remember your promises."

Jon frowned as he considered her warning. Promises? Lord, he'd made so many of them in order to persuade her to come along with him he couldn't remember which one she was referring to. The one to treat her with respect? To get their marriage annulled when Stacey got around to honoring their agreement? To keep his hands off her?

He knew he could handle the first few promises, and any more he might have made in a weak moment, but the last one was going to be a killer.

THE RANCH HOUSE SAT on a small knoll surrounded by elm and birch trees. Hand-hewn logs had weathered to a silvery gray. Worn steps led to a covered porch where a wooden swing and oak rockers enjoyed the shade. There was a hitching rail out front and a water trough, relics of faraway days. Recently watered rosebushes ringed the porch. A short distance from the house, there was a faded red barn and a corral. It seemed to Alex that the cabin and its surroundings were right out of an old John Wayne movie.

And, in his Western finery, Jon looked like its star.

"I thought you said you had all the modern conveniences," she commented in surprise as she gazed around her. "This looks more like a movie set!"

"I suppose it does." Jon laughed. "In fact, I've rented it out as a Western locale a few times. But the inside is modern enough. Take my word for it. You won't have to rough it." He reached inside the car for her tote bag. "You know, no woman travels this light, especially a newlywed. You might want to say your things are being sent here later. Come on in while I round up the kid."

"Uncle Jon, you're home!" A glad shout, then a slender young girl dressed in worn jeans, a short-sleeved plaid cotton shirt and cowboy boots raced out of the barn. She hurled herself into Jon's arms. "I sure missed you!"

"I missed you, too, partner." Jon lifted the excited girl into his arms, hugged her until she squealed with pleasure. "You know I had to go to Missoula to bring you the surprise we talked about. B.J., I want you to meet Alexandra. Alexandra," he announced proudly, "this is Belinda Joan."

"Hello, Belinda. I've been looking forward to meeting you." Alex closed the distance between them and smiled at the girl. Under a series of smudges, she could see slender features that held a promise of beauty and questioning eyes the color of coffee. She had hoped to see an answering smile of welcome. The only thing she saw was a puzzled expression.

"You can call the kid 'B.J.' just like the rest of us do." Jon set her back on her feet with a fond squeeze of her shoulders.

"May I call you Belinda?" Alex asked after a moment's reflection. "It seems a more appropriate name for such a lovely young girl as you."

"I don't mind." A sad smile quickly passed over Belinda's face. "My mother used to call me that. It was my Dad who gave me the nickname."

"Then Belinda it is," Jon agreed. He took a deep breath and announced, "Alexandra and I got married yesterday, partner."

"Alexandra?" Belinda's gaze swung from Alex to her uncle. "I thought you said you were going to marry someone named Stacey Arden?"

"Yes, well, I did. By proxy." Jon hesitated. His new bride's quirked eyebrows dared him to be able to explain the muddled marriage. He would, but he was damned if he was going to explain it all. "I brought

Alexandra home with me because things changed when Stacey couldn't come home from Europe. I didn't tell you about the change in plans because I wanted to keep it under wraps. I figured there was no use in worrying you.''

''Are you going to pretend to be my new mother so the adoption agency will let me stay with Uncle Jon?'' Wide brown eyes gave away Belinda's fears as she nestled closer to Jon.

Alex understood how much the girl needed the security Jon provided. After losing her parents, Jon was all the family she had. But it couldn't have been easy for an orphaned child to face sharing the man she called uncle with a stranger. Or to accept a new mother. Not even on a temporary basis and not even in a game. But Alex was prepared to try.

''No. Only your Aunt Alex and only until your adoption is approved. But I would like to be your friend as long as I'm here. Do you think you might be able to try?''

''Okay.'' Belinda looked up at Jon. ''Does that mean Stacey isn't coming?''

''I don't know for sure. But let's take one day at a time, shall we?''

Jon was nonplussed. He wouldn't need Stacey's help if the adoption went through immediately. The trouble was he hadn't been able to call her off after he'd discovered he was married to someone else. His only hope was to have the court in Billings approve the adoption right away and the caseworker off his back before he had to face the possibility that Stacey might come home unexpectedly.

A smiling middle-aged woman came out of the cabin and down the stairs in time to overhear the conversation. "Well, it's about time you two got home. That child has been on pins and needles every minute you were gone! Asking every few minutes if you'd called."

She smiled at Alex. "Welcome home. I expected Stacey Arden, but under the circumstances, I suppose I should call you Mrs. Waring. I'm Anne Llewellyn, a neighbor of Jon's." She laughed at the way Alex glanced around at the miles of open prairie. "Out here, anyone within twenty-five miles is considered a neighbor. I usually come in twice a week to help out, but I've been keeping B.J. company while Jon went to fetch you."

"This is Alexandra Storm, Anne. But you're right— Alexandra's been a Waring since yesterday afternoon when she agreed to the proxy marriage I told you about." He smiled his apology at Alex. "I'm afraid this marriage business is all too new for me."

Anne Llewellyn looked back over her shoulder. "Not that it makes a difference what your bride is called, considering the circumstances you told me about. Or does it?" she asked Jon.

Feeling like a fool, Jon explained again that there'd been a change in plans. "I suppose I should have told you and B.J. before this, but I wanted to keep it low-key. The rest of the plan is the same, though. Alexandra is going to stay with us until the adoption goes through."

"I don't know how you're going to keep such a lovely young lady a secret, Jon Waring, but you're welcome to try!" Anne laughed.

Lovely lady. Jon glanced over at the woman who was his wife. The last glow of the setting sun framed her fine features, shot golden streaks through her glistening brown hair and put a blush on her cheeks. Her eyes were full of humor as she seemed to dare him to figure a way out of the corner he'd painted himself into. He was surprised at his reaction to her. He had to watch it, he told himself. He might jeopardize everything if he let himself think of her that way.

When he moved to Alexandra's side and touched her cheek, it was purely an instinctive reaction. He'd been drawn to touch her much as he would have touched a floral painting to see if it were real. When his fingers slid down her warm, silken skin, he stopped thinking of her as a temporary distraction.

In spite of knowing better, he wondered how she would feel in his arms. To taste her honeyed lips, see her eyes darken with pleasure as they exchanged the deep kiss he ached to share with her. He had the strangest feeling she was the woman he might have been waiting for, if he had been waiting for one at all.

She was also the woman he intended to say good-bye to.

In spite of knowing she meant nothing more than a convenience to him, Alex found herself responding to the sensual yearning she read in his gaze. For a freedom-loving man who evidently thought marriage was a trap, Alex mused dimly through a rising tide of sensation, he was doing pretty well at playing a loving husband. Too loving, she decided as a flash of warmth shot through her.

Too loving, and too dangerous. If it was all an act, he was a darned good actor.

She'd have to watch herself, she thought as he dropped his hand and turned away to his suddenly frowning ward. Every hour she was near this man, Alex had the growing feeling he spelled trouble. And every minute, too. The last thing she needed was to fall for a man who would rather avoid commitment than offer love and security. Except to a small child.

She'd been down that heartbreak road before.

"Well, now that you're home, come on in." Anne Llewellyn cleared her throat. "Wasn't sure you'd make it home tonight, but I've supper warming on the back burner. B.J., you look like you've been in the barn currying your horse again. That poor animal won't have a hair left on its hide the way you carry on. Run on in like a good child and get washed up now."

She waited until the girl reluctantly ran up the stairs before she turned back to Jon. Her look was troubled. "That busybody, Miss Burns, from the children's court called again. I told her yesterday you were off on a few days of honeymooning, but she said to remind you to call as soon as you got back so she can come over and meet the missus. Oh, and she commented on the convenient timing of your marriage. I'm afraid she suspects something, Jon. Be careful."

"Thank you, Anne. I hope you're wrong." Jon scowled as he replied. "Things are pretty touch and go as they are. I sure don't need any more problems. Well, there's nothing to do but wait until the tough

Miss Burns gets here. We'll take one day and one problem at a time."

He glanced at Alex, started to say something, then seemed to reconsider. "We'll be in in a minute, Anne. Just need to get a few things out of the car. Oh, and by the way, thanks for staying over. I'd appreciate your coming back tomorrow so that you can help Alexandra get settled in. I don't know what I would have done without you."

Jon ran his fingers through his hair when she nodded and went into the cabin. "Damn! What a mess! When I first heard I had to have a wife in order to adopt the kid, I thought I'd convinced Miss Burns this marriage was already on the books! That woman must have a crystal ball."

"I don't see why the adoption is contingent on your being married anyway," Alex said. "Why, in Chicago, I hear of all kinds of adoptions getting approved. Giving the children a loving home should be the determining criterion."

"Well, Alexandra, Montana marches to a different tune about adoptions and lots of other things. Except for proxy marriages, we're probably more conservative out here than most states. Comes from our pioneer heritage. Whenever possible, the courts in the state are big on the traditional family."

"Maybe things aren't as bad as you think." Alex glanced over at the cabin. "How much of the real story do Belinda and Anne know?"

"Enough. At least, they know I meant to marry Stacey and have a proxy bride. I haven't had a chance to tell them we were actually married by mistake and that you're really my wife.''

''For now, and only on paper. Just remember that. I hope you didn't give Miss Burns your future wife's name, or she's bound to realize something's wrong,'' she reminded him.

''To tell the truth, things have been so hectic around here lately, I don't recall. But if I did, I'm a dead man!''

IT TOOK A FEW MINUTES for Alex to orient herself to her rustic surroundings the next morning. At home, she would have been awakened by the sound of raucous automobile horns as motorists fought for an asphalt inch, the hum of elevators and the babble of voices. The silence of the ranch was a new world, and one that would take some getting used to.

She'd grown up in a modest neighborhood of Chicago and, as an adult, lived and worked in a high-rise concrete jungle before deciding to seriously pursue a career as a writer. Nothing had prepared her for the life she was being asked to live now. And never in her wildest dreams had she expected to wind up playing at being a wife with a ready-made family on a Montana ranch.

Aware of Anne Llewellyn's thoughtful gaze before she'd finally said good-night and left for Laurel, Jon had shown Alex to a large bedroom downstairs. And had told her he was going to sleep upstairs and would join her in the morning.

The look in his eyes had suggested he would have joined her if she'd given him a sign that he would be welcome. She knew better. *Never start anything you can't finish,* she could hear her father say. This was something she couldn't finish. They'd already agreed she'd be leaving in a few days or, at the most, a week.

She sat up in bed and hugged her knees while she surveyed the bedroom. Beside the ample maple bed, there was a large wardrobe, a desk, a comfortable armchair and a table beside it covered with books. An antique handmade quilt covered the bed, the wedding ring pattern. As she fingered the tiny, even stitches, she wistfully wondered who had been the young bride who had stitched her dreams and hopes into the quilt.

She glanced at the empty pillow beside her. The quilt's original owner would surely never have dreamed that it would someday cover an abandoned bride on what should have been the first night in her marriage bed, a loving husband beside her. The realization that it was the second time she'd been literally abandoned at the altar shook her out of her reverie. It was time to begin fulfilling the financial agreement she'd made with her husband.

Husband. At the thought, she recalled their night at the hotel in Missoula. Their wedding night. And the runaway thoughts that had kept her awake until almost dawn. She had to stop thinking along those lines. This was just another job, after all.

Male belongings strewn around the bedroom clearly indicated this was his room. The thought that he might come back for his things sent Alex scurrying out of bed. Wrapped in a man-size bathrobe she found in the wardrobe, she set out for the bathroom. She opened the door without knocking and was mortified to see Jon standing there, shaving.

The sight of him—nude except for the towel wrapped loosely around his waist—startled her. His bronzed skin glistened from a recent shower; muscles popped across his taut chest. A tiny patch of blood-stained tissue covered a spot on his chin where he'd nicked himself. Droplets of water clung to the nape of his neck. While she watched, one slid slowly down his back. Her fascinated gaze followed its downward path to below his waist until it disappeared into the towel that rode low on his lean hips.

Mesmerized by the crystallike drops of water, she couldn't think clearly. His smooth back was fascinating, inviting. She started to reach out to touch him to see if he felt as good as he looked, but caught herself in time before she made a complete fool of herself. She put her hands behind her back. Looking up, she made eye contact with him in the cabinet mirror.

"Well, do I pass inspection?" he asked dryly as he finished the last stroke and rinsed the razor with a flourish.

"What are you doing in my bathroom?" she demanded, brought up by her father to believe the best defense is a good offense. His reaction did little to diminish her embarrassment.

"I should think it's pretty obvious, but if there's any doubt in your mind, I'm shaving. As for my using this bathroom, it's the only one around. There's never been a need for another one until now. I'll be through in a minute."

"I'm sorry," she said in a choked whisper, "it's my fault. I should have knocked."

She inched backward to the door. Damn, she was going to have to stop behaving like a smitten school-girl around this man.

"That's okay, I don't mind sharing." He grinned at her through the mirror. "Isn't that what husbands and wives do?" He winked at her before he calmly rinsed and toweled his face.

Only her borrowed oversize slippers kept her from exiting gracefully. All this talk of husbands and wives and intimate bathroom scenes shook her earlier resolve to keep things on a purely platonic plane. And to make him remember his promises. Not that she was in any condition to remember just what they were, herself.

"With those bedrooms upstairs, I never dreamed there'd be only one bathroom. I hope you don't think I crashed in here on purpose."

Jon's knowing glance sent waves of warmth through her.

He seemed to take pity on her embarrassment. "The cabin was built before there was indoor plumbing. Mom had this room made into a bathroom for our use when I was born. But there's an outhouse around back, if you'd rather not share."

She couldn't believe she was playing this ridiculous scene with a half-naked man in a damp towel that left very little to her imagination. A towel held in place by nothing more than a miracle. The interest in his eyes as he took in her disheveled appearance reminded her she didn't have too much on under her own voluminous robe, either. She would have left for the out-house with dignity, but the sudden need for a long, cold shower kept her glued to the spot. She assumed her most ladylike stature and waited for him to be a gentleman and leave.

She involuntarily jumped when Jon brushed against her on his way out of the small steam-filled room. His warm, wet and bare shoulder made contact with her cheek. At her reaction, he laughed, took her by her shoulders and set her out of the doorway. A finger strayed to the dimple in her chin as he leaned toward her. His warm breath whispered in her hair. "Don't forget to wash behind your ears."

She rubbed her chin with the back of her hand and tried not to gaze after him. She could still feel the warmth of his skin and his teasing finger as they'd slid across her face. The pungent odor of his shaving lotion remained behind him in the room and set her thoughts along paths she'd rather not contemplate.

He was a husband only on paper. She knew that. So what sort of power did he have over her that just by touching her he could send waves of electric shocks coursing through her?

She glanced at the staircase where his long, muscular legs were taking two stairs at a time. And, just before he disappeared from sight, she saw the towel fall to the floor.

Chapter Six

B.J. wandered into the kitchen where Alex was setting the table. Anne Llewellyn was dishing up breakfast.

"Alex, why didn't Uncle Jon sleep with you last night?"

The cutlery in Alex's hand clattered to the floor. She glanced from B.J. to where Anne was frozen in the act of setting out platters of ham and scrambled eggs. The two adults exchanged helpless glances.

"Under the circumstances, I suppose he didn't think it was the right thing to do," Alex managed to answer before she dropped to the floor to pick up the scattered knives, spoons and forks. She realized that a child of twelve would be aware of sleeping arrangements between married couples, but surely Belinda knew it was all a masquerade to fool the adoption agency.

Why would she ask such a question anyway? And how were she and Jon going to be able to keep up the pretense of a normal marriage if B.J. might inadvertently blow the lid off their cover with her questions?

And how would an already suspicious social worker approve an adoption if she somehow heard that the newlyweds were sleeping apart? Hoping against hope that her answer would stem the tide of questions she could feel in her bones were coming, she searched under the table for an elusive spoon and knife.

"Maybe he didn't think it was the right thing to do, but it is," the girl persisted, seemingly oblivious to the uncomfortable silence that filled the room. "My dad slept with my mom. All married people are supposed to sleep together, except when they're going to get a divorce like my friend Stephanie's folks did."

"In a way, you're right," Alex said from under the protection of the table. "But in our case, I only came here to help you and your uncle."

"Now, B.J., Alexandra is actually only company," Anne Llewellyn interjected. "She's here to do you and your uncle a favor. Talking about sleeping arrangements isn't any of your business. You should be grateful to her for coming here at all."

"Sure," the young girl insisted. "I know she's going to help us fool the adoption agency. But we can do okay without her after that. She's only staying until the adoption agency checks us out. Uncle Jon told me so."

"That's enough, young lady! Now, get the orange juice out of the refrigerator and mind your tongue. I don't know what's come over you," the housekeeper grumbled, "but Miss Burns had better not hear any of this."

Alex groaned as she reached for an errant spoon. Although she could understand that the girl perceived her as a threat of the unknown, she hadn't anticipated her anxiety would be so deep. But if Miss Burns heard B.J.'s remarks, the game would be over.

"Good morning, ladies," Jon's cheerful voice preceded him. "Breakfast ready? I'm starved." Alex heard the clink of a glass as he must have poured himself some orange juice. "Where's your Aunt Alexandra?"

"Uncle Jon..." B.J. wasted no time in repeating her question.

Glad to be hidden from Jon's view, Alex peered from under the table. Her eyes traveled from Jon's boots past his Western jeans and shirt to his newly shaven face. Tall and virile, smelling of shaving soap, he looked every bit as interesting and dangerous as he had when they'd met in the bathroom. And just as taken aback as she herself had been at Belinda's concerns.

She sank back and waited for Jon's answer.

"Well, sweetheart..." He hesitated when he heard a noise under the table. Bending, he met Alex's chagrined gaze.

"What in heaven's name are you doing down there?" he questioned as he knelt down beside her.

"You wouldn't believe me if I told you it was an accident, would you?" Alex muttered under her breath as she picked up the last of the spoons. She winced as she retrieved a fork from under her hip. "No, I guess not," she added as he looked at her from under raised eyebrows. She scrambled to her feet, tripped on a knife and fell into his arms.

"Here, let me help you!" Jon caught her under her arms and held her to him. "What kind of accident are you talking about?" Brushing her hair aside, his worried gaze roamed over her. "What accident? Are you hurt?"

"Don't ask," Alex groaned, steadying herself against him. She couldn't bear to mention her wounded bottom, not in present company, if ever. And not when the strong arms that held her close fulfilled a fantasy she'd been suffering from ever since she'd seen the towel drop away from his hips. He felt every bit as firm and masculine dressed in his Western clothing as he'd looked then. And just as inviting.

She cleared her throat. "Breakfast will be ready as soon as I get clean knives and forks."

"Uncle Jon?"

"Yes, sweetheart?" Jon kept a wary eye on Alex as she limped to the sink and returned with clean utensils. He could count the number of times he'd touched her. Only twice, or had it been three? Not nearly enough. Their brief contacts made him hunger for more.

Heaven help him, he thought as he tried to concentrate on what B.J. was saying. He wanted to kiss the nape of Alexandra's neck, slide his fingers through her curly brown hair, trace the vein throbbing at her throat with his lips. Most of all, he wanted to press his lips to hers, to taste the honey of her mouth. The fact that she was now his wife, even if in name only, simply served to whet his appetite.

There must be something wrong with him, he decided. He knew from experience he had an impulsive, spontaneous nature, but wanting a woman he'd only met two days ago was nothing short of ridiculous. What he knew about her wouldn't fill a printed page, but he had already sensed she was an old-fashioned type of woman. And certainly not the kind who would go for an affair.

An affair? Good Lord, what was he thinking of? He had promises to keep. Promises to B.J. and to her deceased parents. And to Alexandra, too. He had no business letting his errant thoughts wander along such a torturous path. He reached for the glass of ice-cold orange juice to cool off.

He reluctantly turned his attention, if not his gaze, back to B.J. "What was that you asked me?"

"I asked you why you didn't sleep with Alex last night?" she repeated. It was more of an accusation than a question.

Jon watched a blush creep over Alexandra's face. Worse yet, he heard Anne smother a groan. One thing was becoming evident: he'd outsmarted himself when he'd thought of the proxy marriage and overlooked its possible consequences. Or B.J.'s naive remarks.

Bent on fooling the adoption agency, he had wound up fooling himself. He'd gotten himself a bride and, although he intended to only play at being a husband, he'd behaved stupidly by ignoring the obvious. Judging from the kid's question, and, he suspected, more just like it to come, there was trouble ahead. Especially if she asked them at an inconvenient time.

Stricken dumb, Jon could only stare at B.J.

"Alex wasn't sure, either. But I suppose it's okay."

It was okay with him, too. But not, from the look on her face, with Alexandra. Physically she kept him at arm's length. But his thinking about holding her in his arms and making love to her was something she had no control over. The thought was positively sinful. He didn't know how Alexandra felt, but as far as he was concerned, he felt guilty as sin.

He glanced over at her as he took his seat at the table. So B.J. thought he should act like a loving husband, did she? If the kid only knew, as far as he was concerned it was too late to think of Alex only as a stand-in mother. He already thought of her as a great deal more than that.

"I'm afraid you'll just have try to understand, sweetheart. Alexandra came back with me to do us a favor. Just like I said. But as for sleeping together, well, that's between Alexandra and me. But we have to watch what we say and do. We can't afford to have Miss Burns suspect this is all an act."

"But she will if she finds out you don't sleep with your wife, won't she?"

"How would Burns know, anyway? Besides, Alexandra's not my..." Jon choked on his orange juice. He'd never lied in his life and he wasn't about to start now. Especially to B.J. She deserved an uncle she could trust. "She won't find out if you don't tell her," he warned.

"I won't tell, but I'm not the only one around here, you know. So, I guess you'll have act more married until she leaves," B.J. said reluctantly, giving Alex a cool stare.

"Well, I'll discuss it with Alexandra tonight," Jon said. "In the meantime, let's eat. But you have a point there, you never know when Miss Burns might show up." He studiously avoided his bride's suspicious gaze.

Tonight echoed in his ears. It was a good thing he had a positive attitude and a strong sense of humor. He hoped Alexandra did, too. Between them, they were in a position from which there was no retreat. He had to share her room, he told himself righteously. If he read her reaction to his pronouncement correctly, he was headed for deep trouble. He hoped she would eventually see the touchy side of their situation. Otherwise, marriage, pretend or real, was going to be a risky business.

"Everything is going to come out all right," he said reassuringly. He rumpled B.J.'s hair as she slid into her chair. "It's just something we may have to do for a while, right, Alexandra?"

His worried gaze rested on B.J. as he spoke. She wasn't just a kid anymore, not if she was so aware of marital sleeping arrangements. That was becoming obvious now that he was taking the time to really see her. He'd forgotten how big she'd grown in the past few months. And how feminine she was becoming under the thin cotton shirt and blue jeans she wore. That she might be aware of marriage and what it entailed came as a shock. Should he be asking Alexandra to talk to her?

"We'll see," Alex remarked as she joined them at the table. "I'm sure everything is going to turn out just fine." In for a penny, in for a pound, Alex thought grimly as she poured freshly perked coffee. No matter how she felt about the institution of marriage and its obligations, it was up to her to play the loving wife and new mother for the child's sake. She'd given her word and she took pride in never welshing on a promise.

The only trouble was that speculative glint in Jon's eyes and that sensuous half smile of his as he considered her over the rim of his coffee cup. And her instinctive physical reaction to that look.

Then, too, there was that one bed in the downstairs bedroom that bothered her. If Jon thought he was going to share it with her now instead of sleeping upstairs as he had last night, he was badly mistaken.

"How would you like to go into Laurel, shopping with us today, partner?" Jon pushed away his half-empty plate and drained the last of his coffee. "Your aunt here is in dire need of proper ranch clothes."

"No thanks, Uncle Jon. I get to ride out with Rusty today. You promised."

"Who's Rusty?" Alex inquired. "A horse?"

"No." Jon grinned as he explained to Alex. "He's the ranch foreman. Used to be a redhead, but he's gotten a little older so the boys joke about it. We were going to ride the fences this morning, but you sure need new duds. Maybe it would be okay if B.J. went along without me this time. What do you think?"

Alex was pleased and surprised at the question. Even if she'd been called upon to only play at being Belinda's new mother, it was still rewarding to know she was going to be included in decisions affecting the girl instead of being ignored. Jon was treating her as if they were a real family. She'd play the part.

"Wouldn't you like to come along and buy some pretty dress-up clothes for yourself, Belinda?"

"I had some dress-up clothes my mother bought for me, but I grew out of them. I don't need anything like that around here." Belinda drained the last of her milk and pushed her chair back from the table. "Anyway, I really like wearing jeans."

"What in heaven's name would the kid do with 'pretty things' around here?" Jon inquired as he watched her rush out of the kitchen. "They'd be as much out of place on a ranch as your..." His voice trailed off as Anne Llewellyn cleared her throat. He saw a grim look come over Alex's face. He'd done it again!

"Belinda needs some girl things and maybe some Sunday dress-up clothing. It can't wait much longer," Alex answered firmly. If she had her way, she vowed to herself, Belinda would look like a young girl and act like one by the time the already-suspicious Miss Burns showed up to check Alex out. And, definitely, in time to satisfy the woman and get her off their backs before Stacey came home to further confuse the problem.

DURING THE SIX-MILE DRIVE across verdant grasslands to Laurel, Alex's imagination played with covered wagon trains making their way across the prairie, U.S. cavalry thundering across the plains to protect migrating immigrants from marauding Indians.

She found another surprise when they reached town. All three blocks of downtown Laurel, lazing in the sunshine, looked like another movie set. The streets were a mixture of asphalt and hard-packed dirt, the sidewalks wooden planks. Small wooden buildings housed a Wells Fargo bank, a saloon, a barbershop with a revolving striped pole, a dry goods store and a small hotel with a balcony and a hitching rail out front. Jon stopped at a weathered wooden building, the chamber of commerce.

"We'll just be here a minute," Jon explained. "I need to pick up some papers."

Dressed in his blue jeans, cowboy shirt, boots and a leather belt with a pewter buckle of a bucking bronco, Jon looked ruggedly handsome. A younger version of Gary Cooper, right out of the Western movie *High Noon.* He looked so authentic, she involuntarily glanced to see if he'd added a gun to his outfit. Her gaze drifted downward, imagining a pistol hanging from a loose gun belt that hugged his waist and was tied to a muscular thigh. There wasn't, but that didn't keep her from appreciating the view. Half expecting to hear sweeping Western music in the background, she glanced around to see if the bad guys were sneaking up for a showdown.

Every nerve in her body was aware of Jon's magnetic personality. She felt like Grace Kelly at high noon meeting her man. It was all she could do not to rush into his arms and beg him not to go out into the street and take the chance of getting shot.

When she followed him, she could see a scarred oak desk and chair, a battered wooden hat tree with a shiny brass spittoon and a worn leather couch. A jail cell took up one corner. Her eyes widened. "What on earth is a jail doing in here?"

Jon dismissed the barred cell with a shrug. "This used to be the city jail. We still use it as a holding cell when tourists get out of line. Doesn't bother them a bit. They seem to love getting locked up, even having their pictures taken."

"We?" she echoed, assuming he meant the local townspeople.

"Me, I should have said. I'm the law around here."

"You mean you're the local sheriff, too?" Alex could hardly believe what she was hearing.

"Nah. Only a deputy." He grinned down at her. "It's a dangerous job, but someone has to do it."

"My goodness, everything around here looks like we're in a Western movie."

"Tut-tut, Alexandra. You're beginning to sound like an Eastern tourist."

Alex shivered at the roguish look in his eyes. "An Eastern tourist is exactly what I am, and all of this is too much culture shock." She glanced at the woman dressed in a sprigged muslin eighteenth-century costume seated near the door.

The chamber secretary, who had been avidly listening to the conversation, lowered her eyes, gathered her belongings and made for the door. "Don't mind me, folks, I'm out of here."

"Thanks, Clarice. But we're just leaving." He glanced at the day's mail and threw it back onto the secretary's desk. "Come on, Alexandra. You're next on my list."

They walked across the street to the old-fashioned dry goods store. The windows were covered with vintage hand-printed signs advertising the latest fashions direct from Boston. Once inside, Alex was taken aback by household antiques and nineteenth-century clothing hanging on the walls.

"You want me to wear a costume?" She hung back. "I'm afraid I'm not the type."

"Not at all." Jon laughed and steered her to the back of the store. Wooden floors supported tables of modern Western gear of all shapes and sizes. "The front of the store is just for show."

Alex heaved a sigh of relief. With Jon's prodding, she chose jeans and the shirts he insisted were part of living on a Montana ranch. And, when his attention was somewhere else, underwear. More than enough to last her for the few days she expected to remain in Montana. From the size of the stack of clothing he'd urged on her, it looked as though he weren't all that sure Stacey would be coming back anytime soon. She hoped he was wrong.

And the expense! The money he'd paid her for going through the proxy ceremony wasn't going to last very long if he kept selecting more and more clothing and adding it to the growing pile. And as for the five hundred dollars he'd promised to pay her for remaining in Laurel, that was still in the form of an IOU.

"Jon," she whispered, "I really think that's enough. I can't afford any more."

"I'm paying," he answered firmly. "Just consider it a bonus."

As she tried on the first of her new outfits, her heart beat faster. The man waiting for her outside the dressing room curtain was too kind, too handsome and too unforgettable. Her husband. She fought off thinking of him that way. The marriage was only on paper, she reminded herself for the hundredth time, and that's where it was going to stay. As for anything else, she and Jon were as compatible as sour pickles and ice cream.

Still, no less than an actress would have been, she'd been hired to play a married woman, a wife. A state she'd sworn never to be foolish enough to want to embrace again. Not after the aborted attempt with Tim. She would have to try harder to remember she didn't belong here if she wanted to come out of this adventure with her heart intact. As for Belinda and the ranch, while they might represent everything a woman could want, they weren't meant for her.

Jon murmured his admiration when she came out of the dressing room. Blue jeans hugged her slim hips. White socks peeked from under rolled cuffs. Her tapered shirt, tailored cowboy-style, accented feminine curves that set his body on edge. He smothered his errant thoughts with difficulty. He'd sworn to treat her with respect, platonically. Wasn't that one of the promises he'd made?

"Wait a minute, you need a belt." He took a brightly colored scarf from a counter and started to tie it around her waist.

"Here, let me help," the friendly saleswoman offered.

"No, thanks, I can manage." Jon bent to his task. Almost undone by Alex's fresh scent of lemon and honey, he drew several deep breaths while he put his arms around her and busied himself with fashioning a belt. She smelled like a field of summer flowers in his arms.

"Boots," he announced as he reluctantly tore himself away. He surveyed Alex's white socks. "Definitely, boots."

Another moment with his arms around her and he would have kissed her pert nose. And maybe even more of that appealing territory. Knowing that kissing wasn't part of the bargain they'd made, he forced himself to concentrate on her stockinged feet. "You'll need something sturdier around the ranch than those pink heels you were wearing. Betty?" he called. "How about helping out with boots?"

The telephone rang. "Sorry, Jon. You're on your own. Don't forget to straighten the lady's socks, otherwise they'll bunch in the boots. Gotta take this call."

He could hardly trust himself to handle those pristine socks. Not when he was so conscious of the warm, pink flesh underneath. He took another deep breath and cast an appealing look at Alex. She wiggled her toes, grinned and held out her foot.

"Okay." He pulled up a stool and bent to his task. She rested her foot in the palm of his hand and gave him an innocent look. Innocent, yeah! As innocent as a snake out there in the tall grass. She knew exactly what she was doing and how it affected him. He was willing to bet on it. Especially when she wiggled her toes.

Her flesh was warm under the cotton material as he tried to straighten each sock before putting on the boots. He cast a warning look at her. One more wiggle of those toes and she'd have to put on her own boots!

"How are we doing here?" The clerk ambled back to Jon's side.

"Fine," he said, thrusting the boots at Alex after one wiggle too many. As for the clerk, from the expression on her face, Jon knew that Betty Moorhead was dying to know just who Alex was. And why he was taking an obvious hand in choosing her clothes. Damn, he thought, thinking fast. He'd done it again by not anticipating any of this.

Not that it was his fault. Not even a fortune teller could have predicted this scenario when he'd had to resort to a proxy bride. If she was going to be around for any length of time, he had to introduce her as his wife. In small towns like Laurel, everyone knew everyone else's business almost instantaneously. His private life was no exception. He not only had to keep up the pretense she was his wife for Miss Burns's sake, he had to protect Alexandra, too. He didn't want to see her hurt by gossip.

He reached for her hand. "Betty, I'd like to introduce you to my wife. Alexandra, this is Betty Moorhead."

"Wife? I hadn't heard you got married, Jon. When did . . ."

"Day before yesterday, as a matter of fact," he answered before he realized perhaps he hadn't done the wisest thing by giving away Alexandra's identity just yet. But what other choice did he have? "But we'd like to keep it sort of quiet for a while."

"Fat chance! In Laurel? It isn't every day that our honorary mayor and chamber president adopts a kid and *then* gets married." She laughed as she helped Alex into the second boot. "Sounds to me as if you got it backward."

"Yes, well. You know me, Betty. I guess you could say I march to a different drummer."

"Well, congratulations, you two, although I sure would have thought Stacey Arden would be the bride." She beamed at them. "Still, it don't make much difference which drummer you march to, as long as you're lucky enough to wind up with a lovely gal like this."

"Right," he agreed, reluctantly turning his gaze to Betty. "Anything else, Alexandra?"

Alex cleared her throat. Judging from the gleam of interest in his eyes, she didn't have to be a genius to know where Jon's thoughts had strayed. Maybe she'd gone too far in teasing him. And shopping together for clothes was another intimate experience, and may have been a mistake. "Something for Belinda now?"

"Yeah, sure," Jon said, visibly pulling himself together. "Betty, where's the kids' department?"

"I don't think Belinda belongs in the children's department anymore, Jon. Why don't we try for a junior size?" Alex said as she stamped her feet into her boots and glanced inquiringly at the saleswoman.

"Don't get too much call for junior sizes around here," Betty said, and laughed as she packaged Alex's pink suit and shoes and added them to the growing stack of purchases. "We grow 'em big in Montana.

But come over here, we have a few things that might do."

Alex waited until the woman was out of hearing. "Do you think you should have told anyone we're married, or given my name? What are you going to do when Stacey comes home?"

"*If* she comes home. I was just trying to spare you any embarrassment and to keep gossip from getting started. Besides, Stacey grew up here and Betty would know the difference." Jon looked sheepish. "Looks like I put my foot in my mouth, doesn't it? I guess I wasn't thinking far enough ahead when I thought of the proxy thing. I swear, when I advertised for a proxy I really believed Stacey would be back in time to avoid all of this."

"Good luck." Alex waved back at Betty, who was beckoning from a few aisles over. "You're going to have to be a magician to keep things sorted out." She could feel his troubled gaze as he followed her.

Under his watchful gaze, Alex fingered a pink flowered shirt and a matching short skirt. "These might do until we can find something else."

"That doesn't look like the kid," Jon said doubtfully, cautiously eyeing her selection. "Besides, the skirt doesn't look as if it would cover a gnat's eyebrow. And she'd look like hell trying to ride a horse in that outfit."

"It's a starting place. And she won't be riding a horse all the time. Now, hand me that sweater over there." When Jon complied, she held up the ensemble. "There, that looks like something Belinda could wear when she's not off riding."

"Alexandra, if I know B.J., she isn't going to want to wear those things," he warned, handing her a denim jacket. "But if you insist, this looks more like her than the sweater. Actually, I've hardly ever seen her in anything but jeans."

"Well, it's about time you did. And, so should that woman from another planet, Miss Burns. Wait a minute." She hung back and picked up a training bra. "Belinda will need this, too."

She laughed when she saw Jon's reaction. "Face it, Jon. Belinda isn't a kid anymore."

Jon rolled his eyes heavenward, paid for their purchases and led the way out the door. "Come on, I've another errand to do."

"Like?"

"I'm going to check on the shoot-out." He opened the car door. "Hop in."

"Shoot-out?" she said, thinking of the scene in *High Noon*.

"Tomorrow is the Fourth of July. We take our holidays seriously around here. We're having a barbecue and a dance, among other things. There'll even be a TV crew coming in to film small-town America celebrating the Fourth. Take my word for it, you're going to love it."

At the fairgrounds, Jon appeared to be the official town greeter. Alex tagged after him as he walked through the area greeting locals and visitors. He moved with easy, confident assurance, waving in answer to shouted greetings. From the broad smile on his face, it was obvious he was enjoying himself. And from the questioning glances thrown her way, she suspected she was no ordinary object of interest.

Her suspicions were confirmed when a middle-age woman dressed in a red, white and blue costume rushed over to Jon.

"Land sakes, Jon Waring! I hear you've taken yourself a bride!"

Pulled up in his stride, Jon glanced over at Alex and rolled his eyes heavenward before he turned back. "Yes, Mrs. Luzenger, I have. Where did you hear about it?"

"My sister in Missoula called to tell me she read about it in the newspaper this morning. Imagine, you and that little Stacey Arden finally getting married! We've all been waiting for years for the two of you to get together!" She stopped and peered at Alex over her horn-rimmed glasses. "Why, honey. You aren't Stacey!"

Chapter Seven

"Damn!" Jon said to Mrs. Luzenger's rapidly retreating back. "Let's go over to the library for a minute. I want to look at the back issues of the *Missoula Reporter.*"

"For heaven's sakes, why?"

"I want to check out the Vital Statistics page to see the announcement of my marriage application."

Under Marriage Applications of five days ago, Jon found his own.

"Waring, John L., 35, and Arden, Stacey 32, both of Laurel, Montana."

"Well, it looks all right," Jon said as he returned the newspaper to the rack. "I guess the only problem is that the news got out before Stacey came home."

"So you didn't have to give anyone my name, after all," Alex said quietly. "You needn't have told anyone I was your wife."

"Yes, I did. Especially since Stacey didn't come home." Jon squared his chin. "The last thing I'd ever do would be to hurt you. Not even for B.J."

"Thank you for that," she whispered as her heart skipped a beat. He might not want to keep her, but he was watching over her just the same.

"Come on, let's eat." Jon cleared his throat. "You must be hungry by now."

"Yes. I'm afraid I didn't get much breakfast this morning. Not after Belinda..." Too embarrassed to repeat Belinda's question, Alex felt herself blush.

"I know the feeling," Jon answered as he glanced over his shoulder at the frowning librarian. "I never expected her to be such an expert on love and marriage. Or that the news about us would leak out before Stacey came home in a day or two as she promised."

"You've never heard of the Vital Statistics columns in the newspapers?"

"Of course, I took that under consideration," Jon answered as he juggled their purchases. "That's why I decided to get married in Missoula. I figured I was safe enough by marrying in another county. How was I to know Mary Luzenger had a sister who lived there?"

"I'm not surprised at all. I get the feeling that Montana is one big neighborhood anyway. Besides, with your luck, I'm grateful it wasn't broadcast on national TV." Alex grabbed a package just as it was about to topple off the mountain Jon was carrying.

"Not like a big city, is it?" Jon agreed as he opened the car trunk and dropped in the packages. "Don't you know your neighbors back home?"

"Not really. Actually, I'm no different than the rest of Chicago's apartment dwellers. We tend to be too busy to mind anyone's business but our own."

"I'll take Montana anytime, neighbors and all," Jon said as he shoved in one last package. "Big cities sound like lonely places."

"I never thought about it that way before," Alex answered, "but I guess you're right." She gazed around the main street of Laurel. "It's kind of nice having everyone know you," she said wistfully.

"Yes, most of the time. But not now. Come on, let's eat before my ribs dig holes in my chest."

Alex's eyes were drawn to his commanding torso: broad shoulders, muscular biceps and a tapered waist that she'd already discovered covered tanned, taut skin. Her hands itched to finger his chest, and, if his ribs *were* that close to the surface, count each and every one. Slowly, carefully. Until that itch was satisfied.

Alarmed at the sensuous images that flashed through her mind, she focused her gaze on a distant tree. It was safer than looking at him. What she really yearned to do was taste his lips, surrender to the forces clamoring within her that said yes to every unconscious move he made.

Good Lord, she'd fallen in lust with Jon Waring!

"Let's eat, by all means," she finally managed to say. Anything to be diverted from thinking about a glistening wet male body before her own body language gave her away.

The Roundup Café was a relief. It was thronged with tourists. Half of the people gathered for the

Fourth of July celebration tomorrow seemed to have decided it was the place to be for lunch. Pine-topped tables were covered with red-and-white-checkered cloths. Thirsty diners drank from frosted mugs of cold beer. Laughing couples danced to lively Western music provided by an old-fashioned jukebox in one corner. The tempting aroma of grilling steaks filled the air.

The waiters in Newlander's, the restaurant where she worked back in Chicago, wore black ties. In the Roundup, they wore blue jeans, cotton shirts open at the throat and bandannas as neckties. Soft, deep carpets muted the sounds at Newlander's. But here, sawdust covered the floor. The jukebox thundered and voices were raised in good-natured hoots of laughter and shouted conversation. If diners spoke in hushed whispers as they did back home, they never would have been heard.

She was fascinated by the uninhibited atmosphere, even found herself liking it. But she still felt like a fish out of water.

She wasn't sure she belonged here, not even for a few weeks. Not even for a few days.

"Well, what do you think of the place?" Jon asked, looking around him with a proud smile. "It's the most popular restaurant in the county."

"So it seems." Trying hard to sound matter-of-fact instead of showing how lost she felt, Alex buried her head in a huge dog-eared menu.

From the tone of her voice, Jon sensed something was wrong. He took a closer look. She looked so damn cute in her new stone-washed jeans, blue-and-red-checkered shirt and leather boots, he'd forgotten she was a city slicker. That the down-home atmosphere of Laurel and its citizens might leave her unimpressed.

He glanced at his own clothing. She was probably unimpressed with him, too, for that matter. Rather than being taken by Montana's wide-open spaces, clean air and a population where people took time to enjoy life, she obviously favored the concrete jungle of a big city where land was sold by the square inch. Maybe he'd been right about her from the first. Too bad, he thought with a feeling of loss. She might be fun to be with if she let herself go.

Hell, he didn't need a diagram to know that she could be exciting. But it was looking more and more, from her reactions to the ranch and the quaint tourist town of Laurel, that she didn't belong here.

"What's wrong, don't you care for us cowgirls and cowboys?" he asked casually, steeling himself for a negative reply. Why did he care so much what she thought about Montana? he wondered. She was only passing through.

Alex lowered the menu and regarded him solemnly. "You're a long way from being a cowboy, Mr. Waring." She took in the glint that came into his unwavering green eyes, eyes the color of waving prairie grass. And down to where his open shirt moved with each breath he took. "No way are you just a cowboy."

She knew from the disquieting bathroom scene he was six foot three of rugged masculinity. She also knew his body was muscular and warm. Her glance went to his powerful, clenched hands. Hands roughened with hard work. The same hands that had brushed her cheek with a touch as hushed as a soft breeze lingering for a moment before it passed.

And his character. She'd found him to be generous with his time, compassionate and kind. If he was a man of the soil, he was evidently also a man of the people. No wonder they'd made him the president of the chamber of commerce and Laurel's unofficial mayor.

He was the kind of man she'd hungered for in earlier days. She knew better than to give in to her need. He didn't belong to her. She had to tamp down those hungers.

"If nothing's wrong, what's troubling you?" He reached out and pushed aside the menu she was holding before she could hide behind it. "You seem different now."

"Nothing, really. Maybe it's just me. For a moment, I felt out of place, as though I didn't belong here. And that everyone knew it," Alex answered as she turned her attention back to the menu. "I'm sorry I was so obvious."

"You belong, all right." Reassured that it wasn't the setting, or him, that seemed to bother her, Jon relaxed. "What the heck, everyone needs to play and have fun once in a while. Why don't you just relax and let yourself go?"

"Sure. Now, what's beefalo?"

Startled at the abrupt change in the subject, he eyed her warily. Her answer had been no answer at all.

"Beefalo is a crossbreed of buffalo and cattle. Makes mighty good eating."

"You've got to be kidding me," Alex said, and grimaced. "You mean there are buffalo still left in Montana?"

"Now, now. You've been watching too many Westerns. Want to try a beefalo steak?"

"No, thanks. I don't have an adventuresome taste. I'll just settle for baby back ribs and fries." She was telling the truth. She'd never been an adventuresome type before now. Not until the day she realized she'd never dared to smell the roses. And had answered the advertisement for a proxy bride.

"Got it." Jon beckoned a waiter carrying mugs of beer, captured two and placed the order for the ribs, and a steak for himself. Over her protests that she didn't have a taste for beer, he handed her a mug and settled back to enjoy himself. He hoped she'd wind up enjoying herself, too.

He watched her nibble on a rib bone, dip the fries in the barbecue sauce. A drop of sauce glistened for a moment at the corner of her mouth. When she licked her lips and looked for a fresh napkin to finish the job, he gave in to an impulse and leaned over to wipe her lips clean with his own. He wanted to find out what lemon and honey tasted like when it was mixed with barbecue sauce. The relaxed atmosphere of the Roundup Café invited such intimacies, even if she wasn't ready for them any more than he should have been. Not if he didn't want to give her the wrong impression.

"What was that all about?" Alex asked, wide-eyed as heat rose from her middle. "Another quaint Montana custom?"

"No. Just an old Waring custom," he answered with a self-conscious grin. "After all, I am the president of the chamber of commerce and you are a visitor."

"I hope you don't do it for all the tourists?"

"No way. Just the prettier ones like you."

They sat and exchanged smiles.

"Finished?" Satisfied they were both full at last, Jon gazed happily at his empty plate, rose and helped his proxy bride out of her chair. "Beefalo steaks are prime eating, you ought to try one," he said as they wound their way to the cash register.

"Maybe next time."

"Tell you what," he said, his mind on a more important subject. "When we get back to the ranch, I'll pick out a horse for you to ride while you're putting in time."

"Putting in time? You make it sound like I'm serving a prison sentence. Maybe you've forgotten, but you're paying me to do a job." Alex staggered as she was jostled by a pair of dancers.

"Sorry about that, ma'am," a laughing cowboy said as he twirled his partner away. "Get your partner and come on and join us!"

"I didn't mean it that way," Jon apologized to her as he waved the dancers off. He helped Alex regain her balance. "I only meant that you might as well enjoy what the ranch has to offer as long as you're here."

"Forget the horse," she muttered. "Can't possibly ride a horse after drinking beer."

"On one mug of beer?" Jon sounded incredulous.

"You have no idea what liquor of any kind does to me. I have a very low tolerance for that sort of thing," Alex explained as she carefully put one foot in front of another. "My stomach is in a state of shock. Besides, I'm not fond of horses. I have no intention of getting on one again, or any other kind of animal."

"How do you know you won't like it?"

"Easy," she answered loftily. "I'm afraid of heights."

"Six feet doesn't qualify as a height." Jon held her elbow as they crossed the street to his car. She *was* a little unsteady on her feet. He glanced down at her serious face. If she only knew how comical and endearing she sounded.

"To me, it does," she explained carefully. "But it's not only heights. Why, I remember when I was a girl, my mother took me to a park where some guy was taking pictures of children sitting on a horse. I'd never seen a live horse before and I wasn't enthusiastic about getting on its back. The horse wasn't, either. It took one look at me and bit me on the knee. The photographer insisted the horse was only getting acquainted, but I knew better. He didn't like me."

"*He* didn't like you? For Pete's sake, he was only a dumb animal!" Jon could hardly contain his laughter.

"Maybe so, but I distinctly remember having the feeling he didn't like me."

"You're right. He *was* a dumb animal not to like you."

"Anyway, Mom said she wasn't going to waste two dollars, so I had to stay on the sadistic animal. She had to threaten me to make me stay on and to smile for the camera. I remember it well. I still have color photos that show tears streaking down my cheeks."

"Everything is going to be okay, you'll see." Amused and touched by her oddly poignant story, Jon put his arm around her shoulders and kissed the tip of her nose. The vulnerable look in her eyes tempted him to turn it into a real kiss. He was pleased when she kissed him back. The kiss lasted well beyond a kiss of comfort. That pleased him, too.

"When we get home I'll take you out to the barn and let you get acquainted with the stock. We'll find a horse that likes you. I promise. Come on, here's the car. The ride home will make you feel better."

When she smiled weakly, he was ashamed of taking advantage of her obvious distress. What an odd mixture, this Alex Storm, he thought. One day a sophisticated woman, the next a forlorn child. He took her in his arms again and kissed away the sad look on her face. This time, with a depth of feeling that surprised him.

By the time Jon let her go, Alex knew his kiss of sympathy had turned into something more. And, heaven help her, for her, too. After the first lighthearted contact, his lips had hardened, his tongue had slowly outlined her mouth, probing, tasting, arousing nerve endings she hadn't known existed until now. His hands had stroked her shoulder, drawn her closer. His eyes had darkened, their message clear. He wanted her. And she wanted him. She felt herself drowning in a river of desire.

Alex was dazed by the unexpected kisses and way he affected her. Shocked into sobriety, her eyes cleared as she gazed into his. "You shouldn't do that unless you mean it," she said as she took a deep breath. "And we both know you don't."

"What makes you think I don't?" His eyes swept over her and a rueful smile came across his face.

"*I* think you've just gotten carried away again." Shaken by her reaction to Jon's embrace, Alex stared at the man who was inviting her to take risks that frightened her more than she cared to admit.

His knowing eyes stopped at her mouth. "If so, blame it on your inviting lips. Come on, we have an appointment with a horse."

THE CABIN LOOKED DESERTED when they returned to the ranch. A note pinned to the screened door caught Alex's attention.

"It's from Anne. She's gone home and won't be back unless we need her."

"Probably thinks newlyweds are entitled to some time alone." Jon grinned as she handed him the note. "Come on, let's take this stuff inside and I'll show you the horses."

"Only if it will make you happy," Alex muttered, resigned to her fate. "As for me, I'm not so sure."

"It will. You, too. Trust me."

He carried their purchases into the bedroom, dropped them onto the desk and eyed the double bed. "Guess I should sleep in here tonight or B.J. will be after us again."

"*I* guess you'd better figure out something else." Alex followed him into the bedroom. "That bed is mine, in case you don't know. *Only* mine."

Jon saw her set lips. She meant business, all right, but he was suddenly just as determined to share the bed with her as she was to keep him out of it. And he knew why. It wasn't only to meet B.J.'s expectations, nor the possibility that the social worker might hear of separate beds. It had something to do with Alexandra herself. The need to know her better, to hear her funny laugh, to share the stories of her childhood. And, if she would unbend long enough to allow him to, to kiss her again and again and again.

Damn! She didn't look as if she were going to be that generous. Certainly not enough to let him share the bed. He'd have to think of something else. Something that would at least keep him in the bedroom.

"Maybe my old sleeping bag is still stashed away in the barn. I used it when we went camping up at Glacier National Park."

"It doesn't sound very comfortable," Alex said, wishing she could insist he sleep upstairs. It *was* his home, after all. She debated the problem. Sharing a bathroom when only one was available was one thing. At least they could do that one at a time. Sharing the intimacy of a bedroom with one bed was another. It was too close and too inviting. A sure way to get into trouble.

"Not to worry. It's a down sleeping bag, soft and warm. It'll do just fine. Besides, I don't figure I have much of a choice, have I?" The appeal in his voice made Alex feel more guilty, if possible, but she didn't hesitate before she shook her head. She recognized an invitation to trouble when she heard it. And from the hopeful look in Jon's eyes, she heard it loud and clear.

"Let's go, this stuff can wait." Dismissing their purchases, Jon held out his hand. "I'll introduce you to the horses."

"You talk to horses?" Her eyes widened in disbelief. "You're putting me on."

"Not at all. A horse can be man's best friend."

"Don't you mean a dog is man's best friend?"

"Not on a ranch in Montana," Jon explained. "Out here, a man and his horse are inseparable. And sometimes just as necessary to him as his wife."

"Really? Then you should have gotten the horse to stand in as your wife."

"You're right," he said, smiling into her eyes as he took her hand. "Things would probably have been less complicated if I had."

Musing over his odd remark, Alex warily followed him outside and to the barn. He was certainly different from the urban men she knew back home, but here on a ranch in Montana he was infinitely more appealing.

The recently painted barn was old but obviously cared for. A smaller structure stood beside it. Men's long johns, shirts and worn jeans hung from makeshift clotheslines. A small vegetable garden and a chicken coop were off to one side.

Jon followed her inquiring gaze. "That's the bunkhouse and Cookie's vegetable garden and coop. He's a stickler for organically grown vegetables and fresh food, believe it or not. As a matter of fact, he even has a milk cow in the barn. We have about a dozen hands right now. More at roundup time.''

''Where is everyone?'' Alex said, looking around the silent yard. Except for a jackrabbit sprinting across the hard-packed dirt and a female dog loping its way toward the barn, nothing stirred.

''Riding the fences. B.J.'s with them. They won't be heading back until later this afternoon.''

And we're all alone. Her sixth sense heralding trouble, Alex followed Jon into the barn.

''Here you go.'' Jon stopped at the first stall and stroked the black mare's head. ''Missy is as gentle as a lamb. I'm sure you'll like her.''

Alex gazed suspiciously into the mare's unblinking brown eyes. ''I'm not sure I like lambs, either.''

''Aw, come on. Here, I brought sugar cubes along with me. Go on, give her one. She'll be your friend for life.''

Alex hesitantly offered Missy the sugar cube, snatching her hand away as the mare's eager teeth grazed the palm of her hand. ''My God. Do all horses bite?''

''No. They just don't have good table manners.'' Jon smothered his laughter. ''Ready to try riding her?''

''Not today, thank you. I don't want to make a bigger fool out of myself than I did when I was ten.'' Alex looked around the barn when she heard a faint chorus of yelps. They came from the next stall and she moved to check inside. ''Your dog's had a litter, six of them. Oh, look at the way they keep shoving that little one out of the way. It'll never get any milk.''

"It's B.J.'s dog. She sure has her work cut out for her trying to help that little guy get its fair shake of its mother's milk."

Alex knelt down to examine the puppies. "You poor darling," she said, picking up the mewing runt of the litter and moving it closer to its lunch. The nursing mother dog eyed her suspiciously. When the runt's hardier siblings pushed it aside again, she laughed and moved it back to its mother.

"Your sisters and brothers aren't being very nice to you, are they," she encouraged, making reassuring sounds and stroking the nursing puppy's heaving back. She sat back on the floor to watch the banquet.

"I see I'm not the only one to talk to animals." Jon squatted down beside her and surveyed the animals. "I guess that makes us two of a kind after all, doesn't it, Alexandra? You don't suppose we're more alike than we thought?"

Maybe it was the teasing smile that curved at the corner of his lips, the warmth that shone from his eyes that made her heart soften. She did feel a certain kind of kinship with him. And it was more than solely talking to animals. She met his eyes with an answering smile of her own. They shared the need to take care of a vulnerable child, to make certain a hungry puppy got its share of milk.

The feel of his callused hands stroking hers drew Alex out of her reverie. When had he taken her hands in his?

She felt his touch everywhere, warming her, drawing her inexorably to him. Her eyes locked with his, waiting, wanting, hoping. He seemed to sense her longing. He smiled his understanding, drew a few stray curls away from her forehead and gently caressed the place they'd covered.

She instinctively turned into his arms when he undid the first few buttons of her shirt, drew it down over one shoulder and kissed her bare flesh. She sought more of his caresses, of the lips that lowered to cover hers, the male taste of him: beer, steak and the peppermints he had crunched between his teeth after lunch.

She ran her hands over his cotton shirt, which had been warmed by his body heat, inhaled the scent of him, gloried in the hot sweet touch of his lips and tongue, in the strength of his arms around her. Murmuring her own pleasure, she fingered the hair that curled at the nape of his neck. When he bent forward to grant her better access, she slid her hands inside his shirt, caressing his warm flesh and counting his ribs. She felt the sure, steady beating of his heart.

Her body was warm and welcoming as he pulled her close. He wanted more of her, much more. To savor her silken skin, more beautiful than molten gold, to feel her strain against him. Like an addiction, he couldn't get enough of her. He fought for control.

"Jon," Alex murmured, "we have to stop. We hardly know each other. Besides, someone might come in."

"And who would complain about an old married couple making love?"

"This is wrong," Alex said as she struggled to free herself from the arms that held her. "We aren't an old married couple!"

"No, not exactly," he agreed, laughing into her eyes. "Just in the honeymoon stage."

"We're not even really married!"

"That, Mrs. Waring, could be debated." He brushed a stray sliver of hay from her hair and gazed ruefully at her. "At least, we have a marriage certificate that says we are."

She raised herself on her elbows and looked down at him. "I should have known better than to believe in all those promises you made," she laughingly chided. "You don't seem to be able to keep any of them."

"And what about the promises you made to me and Justice Potter?"

"I never made any promises..." Her voice trailed off as she remembered the words. *To love, honor and cherish...to have and to hold from this day forward...* But they weren't real, she argued with herself... Or were they?

Chapter Eight

He was watching her, waiting, his eyes bright. Asking for something she couldn't give. Jon sensed her unease when he saw a fleeting troubled look pass over her face. Brushing his inner turmoil aside, he struggled to cool his mind and body. He met her smoky hazel eyes with a rueful smile.

"Come on," he said, reaching to rebutton her shirt. "Let's get you into the house so you can rest. You look tired." No wonder she was exhausted, he thought with a pang of guilt. He'd put her through a great deal in the past few days. She'd unintentionally become a wife, a temporary mother and now this. Experiences enough to overcome any woman, even someone as game as Alexandra.

Her body felt soft and warm when he picked her up, cradled her in his arms and carried her to the cabin. "Better?" he asked.

She nodded sleepily and snuggled closer. He wanted more of her, but he'd given his promise. He could treat her platonically, if he had to. But just the thought of giving up the woman he held in his arms left him with a feeling of loss.

And there was Stacey to consider. He still hadn't been able to reach her to explain what had happened. Or to call her off. He was afraid she'd come home prematurely to find he'd actually married Alexandra instead of her. There would be hell to pay for his insisting she come back to Laurel to find he had another bride. All she'd wanted was to stay in Europe with her mysterious lover and come back when she was good and ready. He would have gone along with her, but that was before he'd found out that Alexandra was actually his wife.

He'd have to deal with Stacey's anger later. Not that he blamed her, but she'd started the whole mix-up by getting involved with someone and sending the signed proxy marriage application by fax from Paris. And by staying in Europe instead of coming home to tie the knot for the court's sake so he wouldn't have to go through this charade.

"WHERE'S ALEX?"

"Taking a nap. She's had a hard day." Jon looked up from making a sandwich that would have to double for his dinner. B.J., with a smudged face and rumpled clothing, was home from her ride. "You look as if you've had a rough day, too."

"Yep. It was cool. Rusty let me help the men." She paused dramatically. "I think I'll be a cowboy when I grow up."

"We'll worry about that later," he smiled. "But I think you'd better plan on being a cowgirl. Not that you don't look like one already." He gestured to the platter of ham and Swiss cheese. "Think you can settle for a sandwich for dinner? I wouldn't want to awaken Alex."

"Sure, I guess." She paused and rubbed her stomach. "I'm real hungry. Do you mind if I go over and eat with Cookie and the men?"

"Okay, but I think you ought to wash up first. And be real quiet when you come in."

"Thanks, Uncle Jon." B.J. grinned and rushed to the kitchen sink to wash her hands. "I'll be as quiet as a mouse. I have a new Nancy Drew mystery I want to read later."

"Fine. In the meantime, I'll go check on Alexandra."

HER SLEEPY EYES OPENED slowly. The first thing she saw was Jon asleep on top of the bed beside her. A quick glance at her watch told her it was nine o'clock. Good heavens, she thought in deep dismay, she'd slept the afternoon and evening away! She groaned.

Jon awakened with a start. "Are you okay?" His eyes raked her as he came up on one elbow. "I didn't want to awaken you. I thought this afternoon might have been too much for you."

Too much for her! Alex felt a royal blush cover her as she recalled the sensual look in his eyes in the dry goods store when he had fit her with boots. And the moments in the café when he'd kissed her lips clean.

And the interlude in the barn!

She'd almost made love on a blanket tossed haphazardly over a hay-covered floor, for heaven's sakes!

And escaped making a fool of herself only by a miracle. Was she the same woman who had vowed never to settle for less than true love? And with a man who would be hers forever?

The sensible side of her brain reminded her she wasn't actually a married woman, no matter what Jon had said. The look in his eyes when he'd said it had made her feel as if she were going to go up in a ball of fire. That same look was in his eyes now.

It wasn't helping the problem.

Her only hope of coming out of this masquerade with her emotions intact would be to keep him at arm's length from now on.

"We have to talk," she said, sitting up and punching the pillows behind her. "Thing can't go on this way."

"Shoot," Jon said as he put his arms under his head. "I'm all ears. There's no place for me to go, anyway. B.J.'s still awake. I just heard her go up the stairs."

"To begin with, I agree that we have to share this room and try to keep up appearances of a happy marriage." She paused. "Right?"

"Yes," he said cautiously. For both their sakes, he hoped she wouldn't mention the scene in the barn. First, because it would be embarrassing, and, secondly, because just thinking about his glimpse of her bare flesh made his body stir. He couldn't let himself show how much she affected him. He'd promised.

"Does that mean you want me to use the sleeping bag and bunk down on the floor instead of sleeping here in the bed with you?"

"Not at all. All we have to do is to be sensible about things."

"Sensible. Right." Jon mentally ordered his body to listen to the sermon Alexandra was about to deliver.

"I know from what you've been saying since I met you that you'd rather remain uncommitted." He nodded. "Well, I feel the same way. I couldn't bear to be twice burned."

"Twice? You've never been married before, have you?"

"No. Almost, but no." She looked away from the questions forming in his eyes. Instead, she focused on how he'd been willing to use Stacey. She couldn't afford to let that happen to her. Not when he was a threat to her sense of well-being, her need for security. "But when, and if, that day comes, it has to be with someone who feels about love and marriage the way I do."

Jon took a deep breath. "As long as we're being honest with each other, I suppose you're right. Marriage wasn't on my agenda. Not that I have anything against it," he said hastily when she started to speak, "it's just that I'm busy. I have a lot of responsibilities right now, to the ranch and to the town. And, now, to B.J."

"So then, we're agreed. Let's be friends. You can stay in this room and in the bed until I leave. And when this is over, we can say goodbye with no hard feelings."

"Okay." As he returned her earnest look, Jon thought about her quirky sense of humor and the story about the horse that bit her. Physical attraction aside, she was more fun to be with than without. He would miss her.

SHE HEARD BELINDA and Jon's voices outside in the hall. Checking the jeans that fit her like a second skin, and the blue cotton shirt, to make certain all was in order, she braced herself and opened the bedroom door. Focusing her attention on Belinda, she studiously avoided meeting Jon's eyes. It was the only way she could keep her senses from reacting to him.

"Aunt Alex, Uncle Jon is going to take us to the fairgrounds as soon as you're ready. The Fourth of July celebration is going to start in an hour!"

Alex was pleased to see Belinda was wearing the pink flowered shirt and matching skirt purchased for her in Laurel. Eyes sparkling with excitement, her brown hair was caught up in a ponytail. Today, the tomboy had been set aside; she was all girl. Alex was amused to see that, obviously reluctant to part with all of her usual ranch attire, Belinda wore her usual boots on her feet.

"You look lovely, Belinda. So grown up!" Alex stole a glance at Jon. She could see how proud he was of B.J. She wondered if he realized just how grown-up the girl was becoming, and how many changes in her confronted him.

"Gee, thanks, but I'd feel more comfortable in my old clothes." An embarrassed Belinda colored at the compliment. "There's going to be a real parade, with horses and everything. Uncle Jon is going to ride his horse, isn't that cool? I wanted to ride mine, too, but he said it would be more polite if I kept you company. It's too bad you don't know how to ride a horse, we could all ride in the parade together."

"Guess I just got lucky." Alex could have wept with relief. She'd rather be caught dead than on a horse, let alone riding one behind a marching band. "Don't feel bad. It's going to be more fun watching the parade from the sidelines."

"Gee, I hope so. But I really would have liked to ride my own horse." B.J.'s voice trailed away when her uncle put a restraining hand on her shoulder. "Oh, well. Are you ready yet?"

"Why don't you let Alexandra grab a cup of coffee before we leave, partner. We'll get there in plenty of time." Jon urged B.J. out the door. "Go on, we'll be there in a few minutes."

Jon waited until he was certain he and Alex were alone. Taking her hands in his, he said softly, "I don't know what got into me yesterday, but I want to apologize for it."

"Don't apologize, Jon. I thought we settled that last night. I wanted you as badly as you wanted me." She blushed to recall just how much she *had* wanted him.

"As I said last night, I'm not looking for anything more than friendship. We agreed, no strings. Remember?" She started to turn away. She had to, before she gave herself away. Before she betrayed how much she still wanted him.

He remembered all right. The trouble was he remembered a lot of other things, too: smoky hazel eyes, honey-laden lips, warm, flushed skin. And the way she'd wrapped herself around him before she'd called a halt to the proceedings. He had to make one more try, no matter what he'd agreed to last night.

"Are you sure, Alexandra? I know I have no right to ask, but yesterday was something very special. There's no reason we couldn't go with it."

"I can't, I can't afford to get in any deeper," Alex answered as his eyes entreated her. Tears formed in the corners of her eyes. "You promised."

"Agreed," he said, reluctantly wiping a tear from the side of her eye and placing a final light kiss on her lips.

AT THE FAIRGROUNDS, Jon found a shade tree for Alexandra and B.J. and left for his place in the parade. They were joined by dozens of eager viewers, some with folding aluminum chairs. Small boys found the tree the perfect place to see above the crowd. A blare of music heralded the start of the parade.

The Laurel High School band's glockenspiels led the way playing a lively polka. The band members marched to the quick two-step, cheerleaders whirled partners and danced to the music instead of twirling batons. Horses pranced behind the vintage convertible carrying the governor of Montana, his wife and family.

Lovingly decorated floats commemorating Montana's history followed: a settler's log cabin and a family tilling the soil, a miner panning for gold, Indians on horseback and men costumed as U.S. Army cavalry.

A chuck wagon driven by a decrepit-looking cowboy rumbled into view. It was followed by three teth-

ered cattle lumbering along in single file and several
cowboys on horseback.

"Look, Aunt Alex, there's Uncle Jon!" B.J.
shouted, and waved.

Even without Belinda's shout, Alex's gaze had been
drawn as by a magnet to the attractive man who rode
into sight. He rode a black gelding at the side of the
leading steer, lariat in hand, waving his hat at the
cheering crowd. His hair glinted in the morning sun,
a broad smile covered his handsome face as he caught
sight of them and waved back. With fringed leather
chaps over his jeans and spurred carved brown leather
boots, he looked just like the cowboys Alex had seen
on the movie screen. Only as far as she was concerned, far better.

A young boy stood next to Alex. When Jon and the
other members of the roundup crew came into view,
the boy excitedly shot his air rifle in the air.

The crowd surged forward at the sound of shots.
Some onlookers started screaming. Losing his bal-
ance, the frightened youngster staggered back and into
Alex. A look of horror came over his face. She put her
arm around his shoulders and tried to soothe his fears.
"Don't worry, everything's all right."

It only took a split second for Alex to realize how
wrong she was. The lead steer, spooked by the sharp
noise, veered sideways and headed straight for her,
dragging the rest of the token herd with it. Acting instinctively, she shoved the boy and B.J. behind her,
flung her arms wildly and tried to wave the animal off.

She'd never been so frightened, but she couldn't
wait for help. Lives were at stake here, she realized.

This wasn't a movie scenario, it was real! Shouting and lunging back and forth to distract the bewildered animal, she prayed that Jon, or anyone, would come to her rescue.

The crowd scattered, a few brave souls joined her in shouting. The bewildered steer kept coming.

In a flash, Jon took in what had happened and what Alexandra was trying to do. He didn't hesitate. He urged his horse forward, swung his lariat, roped the spooked steer and tied the rope to his saddle. Shouting for the other members of the roundup crew to take his horse and the cattle away from the crowd, he jumped from his horse and headed for Alex.

"Are you all right?" He threw his arms around her and held her to his pounding heart. At her nod, he glanced over her shoulder to where B.J. and the instigator of the panic were peering from behind Alex, too frightened to speak. "How about you, partner. You okay, too?"

When she nodded, he forced himself to control the heat of his anger. He grabbed the rifle from the culprit's hand. "You should know enough not to fire a weapon around cattle," he said to the white-faced boy. It was all he could do not to throttle the kid.

The boy gulped, too frightened to speak.

"Wait a minute, Jon, you're being too hard on him." Alex moved to stand between him and the boy. "He didn't realize what could have happened. He was just excited and got carried away."

"And one of you could have been seriously injured or killed!" He eyed the stricken boy, trying to control the anger that radiated from him. "What's your name, son?"

At Alex's urging, the boy answered. "Cameron Hardy, sir."

"You from around here?"

"I live in Billings," the boy said. "My dad and I came over for the day."

"Then you should have known better than to shoot off a rifle in a crowd. And when horses and cattle are present! You live in cattle country, for Pete's sake." Jon raked his fingers through his hair in frustration. "Where *is* your dad?"

"Here," a hard voice answered. A firm hand turned the boy around. "Every time I turn my back, you get into some dang fool trouble. Sorry, mister," the angry man said, turning to Jon. "I never thought letting him carry that rifle would cause a problem or I wouldn't have let him bring it along. It won't happen again," he said, coolly eyeing his son and reaching for the rifle.

The man's voice carried more of a threat than a promise.

In spite of the possible damage the rifle shots might have caused, Jon felt sorry for the youngster. He remembered being stupid once or twice himself, and the punishment that had followed. He nodded and ruffled the boy's red hair. "Guess he's been frightened enough by this experience, Mr. Hardy. He doesn't need any more punishment than that. Just see to it that it doesn't happen again," he said, addressing the boy. "Or you will answer to me."

"Yes, sir. I mean, no sir!"

"Go on with you now," he said, giving the boy a gentle shove. "Just remember what I said."

Jon's anxious gaze searched Alex from her head to her toes before he finally led her and B.J. away from the crowd. The thought of what could have happened caused icy fingers to close around his heart. "Are you sure you're both okay?"

"Gosh, Uncle Jon. Aunt Alex saved my life!"

"Yes, she sure did." Jon was shocked to think how close the two of them had come to being seriously injured. And how he had underestimated the resourcefulness of his unexpected bride. He'd been certain she wouldn't last a day on a ranch in Montana. That she would be lost without the modern surroundings of a big city. As he watched color come slowly back into her cheeks, he realized she'd not only handled the ranch, but rustic Laurel, B.J. and him, too. And now, this. Without a murmur of complaint.

"Not really, Belinda," Alex said, taking a shaky breath. "It was your uncle who saved us all."

"Well, let's just say it was a cooperative effort." Relieved, Jon put an arm around each of them and hugged them. "I have to go on over to the reviewing stand and make a speech. Would you ladies care to join me?"

"Where's your horse?" Alex looked around nervously. "I'm not sure I want to be around any more four-legged creatures for a while if I can help it."

"Jake took Cinder along with him. He'll take him back to the ranch with the rest of the horses in the ranch trailer. Come on," he said, finally satisfied that she and B.J. hadn't suffered any injury. He tucked her

hand in the crook of his arm. "Let's go over to the reviewing stand."

Jon could feel her hand still trembling. No wonder.
Facing off a spooked steer was an experience he
wouldn't wish on anyone, let alone a tenderfoot like
Alexandra. Filled with admiration, he glanced down
at her face. Another woman might have become hysterical with fright, run for her life. Not this one. She'd
behaved like a bullfighter and had saved two children
in the process.

Could it be Alexandra was his kind of woman, after all?

The governor stood to greet them when they reached
the stand. "Heard you had a little problem back
there."

"Yes, but everything's all right now." Jon briefly
explained what had happened. "I'd like you to meet
my wife, Alexandra, Governor Adams. You might say
she's the heroine of the day."

"You don't say. Well, I'm proud to shake your
hand, little lady. You're a credit to our state."

Alex didn't know whether to be pleased or annoyed, or to risk telling him she was a Chicagoan. But
she did feel patronized. She'd never been called a little lady before, and didn't care for it now. Still, the
beaming smile that covered the governor's face told
her that she'd been handed a Montana-sized compliment. She shook his proffered hand and managed a
weak answering smile.

At Jon's signal she took a seat, B.J. beside her, and
settled down to collect her badly mangled nerves. In
the few days she'd been in Montana, she'd had more

adventures than she'd anticipated and definitely more than she wanted. Chicago was beginning to look more and more attractive.

"Ladies and gentlemen," Jon said into a microphone, "I'm not going to take your time away from the festivities except to introduce our favorite governor. But first, I'd like to welcome you to Laurel's annual Fourth of July celebration. I like to think it celebrates more than our nation's independence. It's a time for families to get together, to meet old friends, to renew acquaintances. To realize how lucky we all are to have each other and to be lucky enough to live in this paradise called Montana. To enjoy what the generations that came before us left for us. Not only freedom, but a wonderful country to enjoy. Guard it carefully.

"Now, here's Governor Adams. Enjoy the day, folks. And behave yourselves. The TV cameras are rolling!"

As good-natured laughter filled the air, Alex's respect for Jon climbed a dozen notches. Quick on his feet, conscious of his responsibility and proud of his heritage, he exemplified the hearty pioneer spirit that had built the West. She realized that Jon's studied simple exterior hid a man with great depths, a man to be proud of.

The woman who captured him—and *capture* seemed to be the operative word—would be lucky.

Parade and speeches over, Jon collected his charges. "Lunch, anyone?"

"Let me guess," Alex ventured as she wiggled her hips and stamped a foot that had fallen asleep. "Beefalo burgers?"

"What else?" Jon cast a wry glance in her direction. If she kept that wiggling up, he wouldn't be able to keep his hands off her. No matter what he'd promised. Flesh and blood could stand only so much. "This *is* cattle country."

"Hot dogs?"

"If that's what you're in the mood for. Tell you what, let's go on over and check out the food concession stands. You'll be bound to find something to your liking."

An hour later, having downed a lunch of knockwurst and sauerkraut and munching happily on hot buttered popcorn, Alex gazed around the fairgrounds. "What's next?"

"Well, there'll be fireworks later on. For now, there's games and dancing. How about you, B.J.? What would you like to do?"

"Maggie Llewellyn's over there with her grandmother. Can I go and stay with them?"

"Don't see why not. But first, let's ask Anne if it's okay with her. Alexandra?"

"Of course," Alex agreed. "Belinda will probably have more fun with someone her own age. If Anne doesn't mind."

Jon led the way through the crowd, smiling and waving off congratulations on the speech and his earlier rescue of Alex and B.J.

"Great speech, Jon. Short and sweet, just the way I like 'em." Anne Llewellyn laughed. "Too bad the governor didn't follow your example. His tongue wags on both ends.''

"Well, there's an election coming up this fall. To-day was an opportunity he couldn't afford to miss. Anne, B.J. would like to spend the afternoon with Maggie. What do you think?''

"Sure. The girls are fine by themselves, and, be-sides, I don't intend to let them get too far out of my sight. Not after what happened a short time ago." She took Alex's hands in hers. "You sure are brave, Mrs. Waring." Her gaze swung to Jon. "Why don't you show your bride the sights? You're still honeymoon-ing, aren't you?''

Alex felt herself blush. Anne may have been only joking, but she was getting closer to Alex's thoughts than she knew.

"Ever been to a celebration like this?" Jon in-quired as he led Alex away.

"No. When I was young we city folks went to parks to watch fireworks. Later on, it didn't seem too im-portant.''

"That's where small towns have the advantage," Jon said, and grinned. "We have the time to remem-ber who we are. I don't know how you can live in a big city and miss all of this.''

"Perhaps so, but cities are where most of us can earn a living." And it was where she'd go back as soon as B.J.'s adoption was settled. To a safe, predictable life. As much as she'd thought she'd be happy to leave, the reality was actually unsettling. There had been few, if any, adventures in Chicago. Nothing to keep her adrenaline flowing. And no Jon Waring.

"Say, look over there. The band is tuning up for dancing. Do you like country and western music?"

"Some. But it always sounds so sad."

"Only if you let it be. Come on. Let's give it a try."

"It looks as if Belinda and Maggie are trying it out, too." Alex pointed out the two young couples two-stepping to the music of a square dance. "Isn't that the Cameron boy with Belinda?"

"Cameron?" Jon thought a minute. "Oh, yeah. The boy who shot off the air rifle. How did they get so chummy so fast?"

"Well," Alex responded with a knowing smile, "it looks to me as if he might have shot off the gun to get Belinda's attention, hoping to impress her."

"He got her attention, all right, and the steer's too. If he tries that again, I'm going to tan his rear." Jon frowned. Cameron what's-his-name sounded too much like himself at that age, impulsive and impetuous. He frowned over at where Alex was pointing. "B.J. sure looks happy, so I guess she doesn't hold it against him. As for me, I'm not so sure. I'll have to keep an eye on the kid."

"Only she's not a kid any more, is she?"

Jon studied B.J.'s flushed face as she danced by. The kid was actually casting coy glances at her obviously smitten partner! To add to his amazement, her new clothing revealed the curves of an emerging young woman. "No, I guess she's not."

"And fatherhood is not as simple as you thought it was going to be, either, is it?"

"Alexandra, you were never more right." He turned to watch the dancers. "I'll have to find a book and

take a crash course on raising young ladies, won't I?"
He shrugged. "Well, I guess they won't get into any
trouble dancing. Come on, it's our turn, now."

"I don't know how to square-dance." Alex held
back. "I'd only make a fool of myself."

"It's easy. Most of it is a simple two-step. As for the
rest, just listen for the caller and follow me." When
she still hung back, he added, "Come on, I'll teach
you."

It was the perfect opportunity to hold her in his
arms. And he couldn't wait one more minute.

Chapter Nine

Two-stepping in time to the music, Alex's thoughts were more on the strong arms that held her than on the dancing. She stumbled. How was she supposed to concentrate on learning to square-dance when warm arms held her and a soft voice whispered instructions in her ear?

"I'm sorry I'm so clumsy. This isn't exactly my kind of dancing."

"It will be before the night is through," he answered confidently. "Besides, no one's looking at us. The whole idea is to enjoy yourself."

She was trying. The music and man holding her made her inhibitions vanish. The solid strength of him as he led her through the steps gave courage. Soon Alex found herself joining a Western version of a line dance. Laughing over her shoulder, she caught the approval in Jon's eyes. For the first time, she felt she belonged.

A moment later, he swung her around until she faced him.

"Having fun?" he asked as he showed her how to twirl around him.

"Sort of," she said, breathless.

"Good." He two-stepped with her along the edge of the platform and laughingly kissed her each time she came face-to-face with him. Each kiss deeper than the one before.

Through the laughter and kissing that surrounded them, it didn't take Alex long to realize that, in its own way, square dancing was no less a dance of seduction than most dancing. Especially when Jon's whispered words of approval set off fire alarms.

She became convinced of it when the music changed to the haunting melody of "The Tennessee Waltz."

It felt so right when she turned around and melted into his arms. She wanted to taste his lips, drink in his masculine scent. Instead, remembering her resolve to keep their relationship on a friendly basis, she schooled herself to smile brightly into his eyes. It was difficult not to respond to the sparkle in his smile. Especially when it might well be the last time he held her in his arms.

As they danced to a slow, soulful cowboy lament, the afternoon blended into twilight. Red, white and blue lanterns were turned on and the crowded dance floor became a mystical fairyland. To Alex, it was a fairyland where dreams could come true. She closed her eyes to shut out the sights and sounds, and Jon's searching gaze.

He held Alex close to him, inhaled her sweet scent and wished the music would go on and never stop. He'd come so close to losing her this morning. And, when B.J.'s adoption was finalized, he would lose her forever. In the meantime, she wanted only his friendship; he wanted more. He wanted her.

Alex sensed a difference in the way he held her. "Is something wrong?"

"Not really," he said, taking a chance and rubbing his cheek against hers. Her skin felt as velvet as a rose petal, its warmth sweet and inviting. "I was just thinking of the red tape and what it's taking to be able to adopt B.J." he prevaricated. He couldn't tell her of his intimate thoughts. After all, he'd promised just to be friends. But if this dance didn't end soon he would give himself away. "Too bad there are the courts and Miss Burns to satisfy."

"But that would mean there wouldn't have been a reason for me here at all, wouldn't it?"

He leaned back to study the fascinating woman in his arms. The faint smile on her face revealed a side of her that made him want to hug her until she cried for mercy. But, if he had a choice, mercy wouldn't be what he'd give her.

The trouble was, every time he started to think along those lines, the nagging memory of his promise got in the way. "Guess you're right," he said dryly as he mentally thanked God for Miss Burns and the need to keep Alex in Montana. "But it's a little too late to be thinking about that. You're stuck with us until Burns gives me her blessing."

So much for thinking Jon had begun to care for her.

Alex turned her head away before he could see her disappointment. Fool that she was, she'd hoped for another answer.

She returned Belinda's wave as she and Cameron swung past them. The girl was a reminder of what this whole thing was about. That Alex was here only as a means to enable Jon to adopt B.J. He hadn't lied about the reason. Ever. He'd been up-front about it from the beginning. The whole charade was nothing more than a game to him. A game of convenience.

If making love was all she wanted, she'd sensed Jon was certainly a man who could deliver. And that he was willing to try. But she wanted more. She wanted a special man who knew the depths of love and commitment. From all he'd said about marriage, that was more than Jon was willing to give. Not that he wasn't capable of love and commitment; he certainly was lavishing them on Belinda. She had no right to expect them for herself.

Nostalgia and old, unbidden memories hit Alex as the music changed to a sentimental country love song.

Her heart ached when the singer lamented of her long-ago fiancé who had left her for someone else. The lyrics hit too close to home. And now there was Jon. Had she been falling in love with him because he was the man she had come to care for, or was it only a yearning for a love she could call her own?

She glanced at him as he hummed to the music and caressed her waist while they danced. He wasn't playing fair.

"I think we'd better stop," she said as she pulled out of his arms. "You obviously don't know how to keep a promise."

He looked at her as if she'd grown two heads. "For Pete's sake, we were only dancing. Even friends do that."

Friends don't caress you, tease you with sensual glances, kiss you. Or hold you so tightly you can't breathe.

Silently she gazed at him until he shrugged and led her off the dance floor.

Alex turned her thoughts to the time when she would no longer be needed and she could leave. She had a waitressing job waiting for her at home and prospects for a career in journalism. A story to finish when this was all over and it would be okay for her to write it. Chicago was safe. That's where she belonged; not in some Western wonderland.

Jon glanced over her shoulder. "Uh-oh. I'm afraid this 'honeymoon' is over and our real work has begun. Don't be too obvious, but take a look over there."

"What? Where?" Shaken out of her reverie, Alex looked in the direction that held Jon's attention. A staid woman stood at the edge of the dance floor watching them, a puzzled look on her face. "Who's that?"

"Trouble. Come on, we might as well meet it head-on."

They were intercepted by a troubled Belinda. "Uncle Jon, Miss Burns is here. She's over there, watching us."

Jon took in the apprehension on B.J.'s face. The happy smile he'd seen there when she'd danced by a few minutes ago was gone. "I know, sweetheart." He put his free arm around her waist and led her and Alex off the dance floor. "Miss Burns just came here to enjoy the celebration like everyone else. She couldn't possibly have known Alexandra and I are back home."

"She'll take me away! What if she finds out Stacey's not here and that you and Aunt Alex aren't really married! That you're just trying to fool her!"

"Don't worry about Stacey, Belinda," Alex quietly reassured her. "For all intents and purposes, your uncle and I *are* married. There's nothing she can say that would change that."

"Ah, Miss Burns!" Jon forced a welcome smile to his face. This was the woman who held B.J.'s future in her hands. "I'd like you to meet my wife, Alexandra."

"Alexandra?" Miss Burns did a double take. Her small mouth tightened as she looked Alexandra up and down. Her questioning gaze swung to Jon.

"I'm happy to meet you, Miss Burns." Alex quickly joined in the conversation before there could be a torrent of questions. "I've heard so much about you."

Miss Burns's thin lips tightened. "Thank you, I'm sure. I'm quite interested in meeting you, too, Mrs. Waring." She turned doubtfully to Jon. "I understood you were going to marry Stacey Arden. Where is Stacey, anyway?"

Not again, Jon thought with an inward groan. Another land mine waiting for him! This time he'd forgotten Stacey and Letty Burns had worked together not too long ago on a story about abandoned children. Would there ever be an end to the details he'd overlooked? It was as if some evil force had taken over his affairs to prove that even the best-laid plans can go astray.

"Well, yes, but my plans took a sudden change. As a matter of fact, Stacey is somewhere in Europe on an exclusive story for her network. Alexandra here took me by storm before Stacey and I got around to tying the knot. Didn't you, love?" He nuzzled Alex's hair, and smiled fondly down at her.

"I guess we just couldn't help ourselves." Alex agreed, taking her cue. "One look and we knew we were meant for each other. I'm sure you know how that can be."

"As a matter of fact, I don't." A fleeting look of envy passed over the social worker's face. "Why haven't you contacted me to let me know you were back, Mr. Waring? I left word with Mrs. Llewellyn to have you call me right away. My supervisor is anxious to close this case and move on."

"And moving on, we are," Jon assured her. Ignoring her quick intake of breath, he kissed his "bride" on her full lips. "With our honeymoon, you know."

Letty Burns blushed and cleared her throat. She met B.J.'s wide-eyed gaze. "And how do you like the change in plans, Belinda?"

"Come on, Miss Burns. Today's a holiday." Jon released Alex and focused all his charms on the lady before B.J. could reply. "Why don't you forget business and enjoy yourself. We can get together and discuss this matter at the ranch on Monday. That's only a day away. That is, if you're free."

"Perhaps Tuesday would be better. I have a number of appointments Monday, but yes, I'll be there bright and early Tuesday morning." She shot Jon a thoughtful glance before she turned to Alex. "I'll see you on Tuesday morning, Mrs. Waring. And you, Belinda. I'll want to talk to you, too."

She threw a speculative look their way before she said goodbye. As she disappeared into the crowd, Jon had the sinking feeling that the lady already suspected he and Alexandra were anything but a pair of star-struck lovers.

"Now, HERE'S THE game plan," Jon explained when they returned to the ranch. "I don't trust Burns a damn. If she said bright and early, she's liable to show up at dawn to roust us out of bed. Alexandra, you and I will have to continue to bunk in together. And you, B.J., don't forget to call Alex your aunt."

Out of the corner of her eye, Alex noticed the way Belinda scowled at Jon's remark. Something was bothering the girl, and she was afraid it wasn't only the prospect of being interviewed by Miss Burns.

"Why don't you go on upstairs to bed, Belinda? You must be tired from all that dancing with your new friend," Alex said in sympathy. No young child should have to put up with the fear of being taken away from the ones she loved. Losing her parents was bad enough. Surely, she wouldn't have to lose Jon, too.

She remembered her own childhood when she'd been taken from a foster home and had found a father and mother. "Would you like to have some 'girl talk' time? Just the two of us?"

"No thanks." Belinda pulled away and avoided meeting Alex's eyes. "Anyway, I haven't anything to talk about with you."

"B.J.!" Jon said, surprised at the surly tone in B.J.'s voice. "Alexandra saved you from a pretty scary situation this afternoon. You should be grateful."

"Well, I am, if that's what you wanted to hear. But I don't want to talk about the dance or any of my friends with her. That's for children, Uncle Jon," she said as she tossed her head. "I'm not a child anymore."

"If you're not a child anymore, then you're old enough to apologize to Alexandra, not to me," Jon said, troubled over the way the situation was going. Something was wrong, but he'd be damned if he knew what it was.

"Sorry," Belinda said defiantly over her shoulder to Alex as she marched up the stairs. "I should have known things were going to turn out this way."

Jon looked uncertainly after her. "I wonder what's wrong with the kid. She's never acted like this before."

"Uncle Jon?" B.J. hung over the railing. "Can we go riding tomorrow?"

"Sure, I don't see why not." He glanced at Alexandra and hesitated. "Do you mind staying here alone for a few hours tomorrow?"

Alex had a suspicion she knew what was bothering Belinda. And since she'd begged off getting near a horse herself, it was pretty obvious to her why the girl had asked to go riding with her uncle. "Since Belinda seems to need to have you alone for a while, go ahead. I don't mind at all."

"Are you saying she's jealous of you?"

"In a way. You *are* all she has," Alex said thoughtfully. "I remember how I felt when I was her age. It's only that most girls worship their fathers. And in this case, you fit the bill."

"That's no reason for her to treat you this way." He was in a turmoil as he glanced at the upstairs landing and back at Alex. "You'd think the kid would know she has as much at stake in this as I do. I'm going up to talk to her and straighten things out. Wait here." He strode up the stairs and knocked on B.J.'s bedroom door.

Alex sighed as she watched him disappear from view. Jon had a lot to learn about fatherhood, especially about raising a girl on the verge of becoming a woman. No wonder the court had wanted a woman in the house to deal with the situation. Considering that Belinda had declared her territorial rights, they were going to have their hands full until this was over.

BELINDA LET HIM IN and, hands on hips, faced him defiantly. "Something bothering you, sweetheart?" he asked.

She hesitated, then burst out. "You don't want me around anymore!"

"Don't *want* you?" Jon couldn't believe what he was hearing. He sank into a chair beside the bed. "What in the world makes you think that I don't want you?"

"Because you've got Alex now."

"Only for a little while, partner," he said, trying to be patient and logical. In spite of her anger, she looked so young and forlorn. He made a new resolve to keep his promises to both her and Alexandra. "You've known that from the beginning. There's nothing for you to be jealous about."

"That's not the way it looks." She faced him defiantly, eyes sparkling with unshed tears. "You treat her like you want her here."

"I thought you liked her." Jon was taken aback. How could he have been so wrong about the way she would feel about Alexandra? Maybe, he thought, hearing the hint of jealousy in B.J.'s voice, the kid wasn't a kid anymore, after all.

"That was when I thought your having a wife was just a game to fool Miss Burns. And that Alex was only going to be here for a few days. Now it looks as if she's going to be here forever!"

"What makes you say that?"

"The way you keep kissing her and talking about honeymoons." Her muffled voice showed she was too embarrassed to meet his eyes.

"That was for Miss Burns's sake," Jon answered, remembering scenes he couldn't afford to be thinking of right now. So, his public demonstrations of affection for Alexandra hadn't looked like an act at all. Nor, to be honest with himself, were they. Not lately, anyway. No wonder Alexandra had taken him to task. He'd have to watch himself and for more than one reason. "Here, look at me." He rose and lifted B.J.'s tear-streaked face. "I wouldn't trade you for anything or anyone in the world. Alexandra only came here to do us a favor."

"*She* said you were really married! I'm old enough to know what that means. And if you are, maybe you don't need me to be part of your family. You can have children of your own."

"Oh, my poor little partner," he said, seeing tears well up. It was no time to tell the truth about his marriage. "I'll always want you to be my family. I can't imagine not having you with me."

Alex had been right, again. B.J. had no one other than him to call her own. With the adoption still up in the air she must be terrified it wouldn't go through. With another woman in the picture to threaten her tenuous sense of security, no wonder she was so afraid. This child was his responsibility. He owed her love, security and happiness. There was no way that he'd risk hurting her. Despite her bravado, she was so sweet and so vulnerable.

"Why don't you get in that T-shirt you call a nightgown and climb into bed. Everything is going to be all right. Don't worry about a thing. Promise?"

"I promise, Uncle Jon." A watery smile lit up her face. "I love you so much."

"I love you too, partner," he said, compassion for her filling his heart. He had to do something about this situation tonight. "Good night, sweetheart."

He went downstairs, thinking about having to tell Alex she'd been right. And, for more than one reason, right about having to cool it. After making love to Alex, teasing her into sexual awareness, she would be bound to think he was making a fool of himself and her. After the way he'd handled the whole mess, maybe he *was* a fool. Certainly he wasn't the brightest guy when it came to understanding women.

"Was I right about what's bothering Belinda?"

"I'm afraid so." He went on to explain the conversation he'd had with B.J. "Darned if I foresaw this kind of reaction," he said, pacing the floor. "She thought it was just she and I together, until you showed up."

"*I* showed up!" Furious, Alex marched up to Jon and vented her frustration. "If you remember, the reason for my coming to Montana wasn't for a real marriage and instant motherhood. Not until *you* played on my sympathy and talked me into coming here! And then spending all your time trying to get me into bed when it was only a game to you!"

She took a deep breath to control herself, but it wasn't working. "You make it sound as if we're two women fighting over the same man! Well, let me tell you something, Mr. Waring. I'm not trying to take you away from anyone, Belinda least of all!"

"That's not what I meant, and you know it." He took a step backward at her clenched fists and blanched at the fury in her gaze. "I just don't want to make B.J. any unhappier than she is. I don't have anything against you."

"Great! I don't know anything more than what I've heard here," she answered. "Even if you meant something else, my answer is still the same! You don't belong to me and I don't belong to you!"

At first, Jon was surprised at what he thought was an overreaction. Until her flashing hazel eyes gave away a greater depth of emotion than what could be merely anger over B.J.'s behavior. This argument had to be over something between the two of them. Had she read more into his sexual play than he'd intended? Had she mistaken a powerful mutual attraction for a promise of something more?

He liked her for more than just lovemaking, it was true, and more than he should have. Somewhere along the line, he must have given himself away. Enough to have given both her and B.J. the wrong ideas about the future. Maybe all of this turmoil *was* his fault, but it hadn't been by design. She had no right to make such accusations.

"Now you've gone too far," he said in a tight voice, trying to keep his voice down so B.J. wouldn't overhear the argument. "What makes you think you have the right to act this way?"

"I'm your wife, remember?"

"Not by any fault of mine," he retorted with a scowl. "And not a real one, either. You were supposed to only be a proxy bride, until Potter messed up." Hell, he thought through a growing headache that had his head in a vise, this was just like arguing with a wife! No wonder he'd never felt the need to get married.

She met him glare for glare. "Not after that interlude in the barn! You were behaving as if I *am* your real wife. Well, let me tell you, if we'd gone all the way the other afternoon, I would be. And, instead of an annulment, we'd have to get a divorce. Not that the thought of being your wife makes me any happier than it seems to make you. You can relax. I'm leaving just as soon as I fulfill my part of the bargain."

He felt like a heel.

At the very least, he owned her an apology.

"I'd like you to believe I never wanted you to get hurt. Not after all you've done for us."

"Don't bother to apologize," Alex replied. "You've never offered me anything more than money for being a proxy mother and an annulment when the job was over. That's all that matters to me."

"Fine. I'll give you a check in the morning." So, Jon thought as he regarded her with his own growing anger. Money *was* the only reason she'd come with him, after all. He'd thought it was compassion for B.J. And, fool that he was, that she cared something for him.

In the morning, a Jeep pulled up in front of the cabin where Jon was about to leave for the barn. Alex, emotions firmly under control, stood watching from the porch.

"Morning, Jon, Mrs. Waring." The driver touched his fingers to his broad-brimmed hat. "Clarice at the chamber office asked me to bring you your mail. She didn't think you'd be coming in today, seeing as how I hear you folks are on your honeymoon. Kind of sudden, wasn't it?"

"Hi, Tom. You might say so," Jon answered, glancing at Alex's closed face. Damn! It wasn't the time and place to continue the argument, but he still had plenty to say. "I'd like you to meet my wife, Alexandra."

"Pleased to meet you, ma'am. You're not from these parts, are you?"

"No. I'm from Chicago," Alex said with a fixed smile on her face.

"Thought so. I know most everyone for miles around. Well, congratulations." He hefted a large box of mail onto the steps. "Looks like you folks are on everyone's sucker list, don't it?"

"Thanks, Tom. It *is* a heck of a lot more mail than usual, isn't it?" A quick look at the first few envelopes turned into Jon's worst nightmare. The publication of his application for a marriage certificate in the Missoula newspaper had seemingly launched a storm of mail from all of the businesses in Montana, and points east.

"Well, see you later." Tom laughed as he said goodbye. "Don't spend all your money in one place."

Jon cursed under his breath as he glanced through the mail. It seemed as if everyone who had read the newspaper was interested in his marriage. He opened a few envelopes and handed them to Alex. "I can't believe what I'm reading!"

She sank into a wooden rocker and started opening envelopes. The first letter was an advertisement from a real estate firm in Missoula offering low interest mortgage rates for the newly married Mr. and Mrs. Waring. Another was from a department store in Billings offering low down payments on a house full of furniture for the newly wedded couple. It was followed by offers for health insurance for the new family, children included. There were applications for credit cards, magazine subscriptions for the new bride, information on family planning, or, if she were already expecting, tips on ensuring a healthy pregnancy.

Pregnancy, of all things!

She stared at the seemingly unending pile of envelopes. Filled with an overwhelming desire to leave Blue Sky immediately, she realized their annulment would show up in another newspaper's statistics column. With her luck, its publication would only loosen a mass of unwanted literature for the newly divorced.

Jon hesitated as he glanced at a final letter before throwing it back into the box. "This sort of thing isn't helping much. Maybe we'd better talk things over when I get back."

"As far as I'm concerned, we said it all last night." Alex let the letters fall back into the box at her feet. "I'm leaving as soon as Letty Burns does her house call and you pay up. And it won't be too soon for me."

Chapter Ten

A distant brisk knock sounded, and again.

"Good God, the woman is worse than I thought!" With a groan, Jon glanced at the clock and bounded out of bed. "I was only kidding when I said she'd probably be early enough to roust us out of bed! I guess I might as well let the dragon in." Jon glanced over to where Alex had flung on his discarded shirt. She was busily rummaging through dresser drawers, looking for fresh clothing. He hurriedly shucked his pajama bottoms, drew on his jeans and headed for the bedroom door.

"Wait a minute! You don't intend to go out looking like that, do you?"

Jon paused and looked down at his bare chest. "Yes, I am. First of all, you're wearing my favorite shirt," he said facetiously. "Secondly, I have a hunch our dear Miss Burns is suspicious about the 'depth' of our relationship. Mainly, are we sleeping together as man and wife. So," he said, eyeing the bundle of fresh clothing in Alex's hands, "let's give her something to think about. Let's be half dressed so she'll know we've just awakened. Together.''

"Together?" Alex paused uncertainly. "Are you sure? Miss Burns impressed me as a conservative type."

"I'm sure. If I were you, I'd just throw a robe over that shirt. Besides," he continued, "Miss Burns could probably use a little excitement in her life." He took a grim satisfaction when she blushed. "And so could someone else I know!"

"Don't say anything more. Don't even think it!" Alex ordered. "You macho men are all alike. Anything to give us poor women a thrill."

"Don't tell me you find my chest thrilling," he said, scowling. "I got the impression that you had enough of me to last a lifetime."

She dropped the clothing she held, snatched his shirt off her shoulders and threw it at him. "Don't even think about it! Now you have no excuse to flaunt your masculine charms."

Riveted to the sight of her lush body outlined by the sunlight streaming through her sheer nightgown, Jon swallowed hard. He let the shirt fall through his fingers and onto the floor. He knew she was angry with him, and as a matter of fact, he wasn't too happy with her, either. But she didn't need to torture him.

"You don't play fair. If flaunting masculine charms is out of bounds, there must be something in those rules of yours against flaunting feminine charms." He glared at her. "Right now, I'd say you're guilty of breaking more rules than I am."

Alex followed the path his eyes were taking. It was then she realized how little she was wearing, how much of her was revealed. Intentional or not, she was leaving nothing to his imagination! Good heavens, she thought as she reached for a robe. The last thing she needed was to provide him with an opportunity to discuss their mutual weaknesses. She'd had enough arguments to last her a lifetime.

The impatient knock was repeated. Jon paused. "If it weren't for our visitor, I'm sure we could fight this issue to a mutually satisfactory finish."

"Keep your mind on business. Go on and answer the door." She held the robe in front of her. "I'll be with you as soon as I freshen up."

"I'll go, but don't think this is the end of the conversation." He dodged as a slipper narrowly missed his head. "See you later. And don't forget to act as if you're Mrs. Waring."

Forget she was Mrs. Waring? Alex was sure it wasn't going to be easy to forget as long as he was around to torment her. Thank goodness the end to this charade was in sight. As soon as he gave her a check for five hundred dollars, Chicago, here she came.

"Ah, good morning, Miss Burns. Right on time," Jon remarked as he opened the door and glanced at his watch. "Seven o'clock."

"I do have other petitioners to visit." His visitor colored and answered crossly as she took in his bare chest. "You might have put on a shirt, Mr. Waring."

"I'm sorry. Fact is, you got us out of bed. I didn't want to keep you waiting. But if this bothers you, I can go finish dressing. That might take a while," he added, hoping the lady knew how to take a joke. "But if you're not in a hurry. . . ?"

"Never mind," she rejoined, averting her eyes. "Perhaps we can get on with this. Where is Mrs. Waring?"

"Probably still in bed where I left her. She seemed a little tired after last night, so I let her sleep." He winked.

Miss Burns frowned. "Mr. Waring! If you're deliberately trying to upset me, let me tell you I've seen and heard a lot more shocking things than marital bedroom activities during the course of my duties. Unless, of course—" she paused, "—you're not actually married after all."

"What an odd notion," Alex interjected. She came up behind Jon and poked him in the ribs. "Behave yourself," she said with a false smile. The man was his own worst enemy. "Miss Burns might think you're serious. Please excuse my husband, Miss Burns."

She was wearing his robe and slippers. With her tousled hair and just-out-of-bed rosy complexion, she was more appealing than ever. It was beyond him how she could look so loving when he was aware of the anger under that wifely facade. It was only when he noticed her incredible hazel eyes were ringed with signs of fatigue that he realized why.

She was trying to cope with changes in her life: their unexpected marriage, a jealous B.J. and sleepless nights. And now, a skeptical Miss Burns. It served her right. If Alexandra had met him halfway in his attempt to do the right thing by B.J., he thought righteously, it would have been a lot easier on both of them. As it was, trying to keep a woman happy was a lot like trying to lasso a steer.

"Jon, why don't you take Miss Burns into the parlor while I put on a pot of coffee. Miss Burns?"

"Thank you, coffee would be welcome." When Jon opened the door wide and gestured for her to enter, the social worker swept by him with an audible sniff. She gazed around the entry, walked over to the adjoining parlor and looked inside.

"This is acceptable," she said, making notes in a small notebook she took out of her purse. "Of course, I'll want to see the rest of the house, also. Especially Belinda's quarters."

Acceptable? Jon gazed around a room filled with heirloom pine and maple furniture, some of it hand-made by his great-grandfather. A hand-tied rug lovingly made by his great-grandmother lay on the floor. Chintz covered the sofa and occasional chairs, hand-crocheted doilies lay on the maple end tables. Family pictures sat on the mantel, hunting trophies hung from the wall. Four generations of Warings had grown up in these surroundings. Surely the lady couldn't have expected anything better for the kid than what he'd grown up with.

"And where is Belinda?"

"Upstairs, probably still fast asleep. You know growing kids need their rest."

"I'll want to interview her before I leave." She continued to avert her eyes while she looked around the room. "And your wife, too."

"Is there a problem?" He gestured her to a seat on the sofa and took a chair across the coffee table.

"Not exactly," she said, studiously consulting her notes. "From the court records, there's no doubt about your financial ability to take care of Belinda Joan, Mr. Waring. Nor about your character, I suppose." She paused and glanced significantly at his bare chest. "You seem to be quite a celebrity in Laurel. However, as you were told earlier, the court's concern was that there was no woman in your home to guide the child into puberty and beyond."

"There is now," Alex commented as she came into the room carrying a tray of steaming coffee and three cups. Jon's shirt was slung over one shoulder. "As you are no doubt aware by now, Jon and I were married last week in Missoula." She laid the tray on the coffee table, let Jon's shirt slide into his lap and fixed him with a cold stare. When he raised his eyebrows, she turned her back on him and poured the coffee.

"Yes, well," Miss Burns said firmly as she leafed through her records, "I'm afraid there'll have to be some clarification. This report says you informed the court you intended to marry Stacey Arden. Your wife is Alexandra . . . ?"

"Alexandra Storm Waring, Miss Burns." Alex answered for him in a tight voice. "I hope you take your coffee black. We haven't had time to shop for niceties."

"That will be fine, thank you." Appearing grateful for the distraction, Miss Burns sipped the hot coffee. "And now, Mr. Waring, back to the subject of your impulsive marriage to Mrs. Waring. What made you change your mind about marrying Stacey at the last minute?"

"I don't know what difference it makes now, but the fact is Stacey and I have been good friends all of our lives. Too good, we finally realized. And not really marriage material. When I met Alexandra, I knew she was the one for me. Stacey understood."

"You've spoken to Stacey about your marriage?"

"Yes." He felt very self-righteous. Proud of the fact almost every word of his statement had been true. He *had* spoken to Stacey about the proxy marriage, even if he hadn't been able to tell her it had turned out to be real. As for Stacey understanding, well, he'd cross that bridge if and when she came home.

"Very strange, indeed," Miss Burns mused, her pencil tapping her pursed lips. "But, I suppose it's possible you could have met, fallen in love and married in the space of less than two weeks." Her narrowed gaze gave away her skepticism. "And you, Mrs. Waring. Where and how did the two of you meet?"

"In Chicago." Alex sat down in a chair beside Jon, carefully closing the robe over her legs. Ignoring his glance, she toyed with her coffee. "My husband goes to Chicago regularly for business pertaining to the ranch. I've lived and worked there all my life."

"Oh? Just what type of work do you do?"

Jon surged to his feet. "What difference does it make what Alexandra did to earn a living? She's going to be a homemaker from now on!"

"I don't mind telling Miss Burns," Alex interjected, with a warning glance in Jon's direction. "I was an aspiring journalist working part-time as a waitress. Jon came in a few times for lunch. In fact, that's how he and I first met," Alex explained, a false smile for Miss Burns's benefit on her face. "Although my husband is correct. What difference does it make?"

"None, I suppose," Miss Burns said, making a rapid note on her papers. "I just wondered what your credentials are with regard to raising B.J."

"Don't tell me my wife needs credentials to be a mother?" Only Alex's restraining hand on his knee kept Jon in his chair.

"Surely you must realize how important it is for the courts to be certain an adoption is in the best interests of the adoptee. Almost any woman can have a child— unfortunately, not all of them know how to be mother."

"Belinda is a lovely young woman, Miss Burns. Not just an adoptee, as you put it." Alex rose and tightened the robe around her throat. "As for myself, I'd be happy to provide you with any further information or references you think are proper. Until then, please excuse me. I need to get dressed."

Letty Burns closed her notebook with a snap. "Of course. And you, too, Mr. Waring," she said, glancing pointedly at his bare chest and the shirt in his lap. "I'm sure you'll want to finish dressing, too. Now, where would I find Belinda?"

"Here I am." Barefoot and dressed in a Travis Tritt T-shirt, Belinda hung back in the doorway. After casting a silent appeal at Jon, her wide eyes fixed themselves on Letty Burns.

Alex put a sympathetic hand on Belinda's shoulder in passing. She'd been in this position herself many years ago and could still remember the hollow feeling in the pit of her stomach as a judge questioned her adoptive parents in front of her. He'd asked if they were certain they wanted to adopt an older child at their age. Childless after twenty years of marriage, the Storms's answer had been a resounding yes. When the judge had finally signed the papers making her their child, her prayers had been answered. After living in foster homes for most of her life, she finally had two loving parents.

Under her hand, she could feel Belinda tremble. She bent to whisper her reassurance and gave her a gentle push in Jon's direction.

"May I speak to Belinda alone?"

"Uncle Jon!" B.J.'s eyes begged him for help.

"Everything's going to be okay, sweetheart," Jon replied. When B.J. skirted the table and sidled close to him, he drew her close. He turned on the watchful social worker. "I'm sure there's nothing you can ask B.J. that you can't say in my presence, Miss Burns."

"Perhaps, and perhaps not. We'll see. Now, Belinda, you're aware your uncle applied for your adoption prior to his marriage, and that the courts held back their approval until he advised he was about to be married?"

"Yes, ma'am," Belinda answered in a shaky voice. She glanced at her uncle and back at Miss Burns.

"To Stacey Arden." She gazed thoughtfully at her notes before looking up. "Do you know Miss Arden?"

"No, ma'am."

Jon could see B.J.'s growing anxiety as she looked up at him. He gave her a reassuring smile.

"You've never met Miss Arden?"

"Come on, Miss Burns," Jon interrupted when he felt B.J. tremble. "She's already told you she doesn't know Stacey. Stacey had moved away to New York by the time B.J. was born. I don't see what that has to do with the adoption?"

"I'll get to that in a minute. So, you didn't meet Alexandra Storm either before she came to the ranch? No? I didn't think so." She made another rapid note in her journal. "Now, Belinda, are you happy living here on the ranch with Mr. Waring?"

"Oh, yes. I've loved Uncle Jon forever," Belinda replied earnestly. "My mom and dad did, too. We used to visit every summer. He taught me how to ride a horse and lots of other things. Now that I've come here to stay, he's even given me my own horse," she said with enthusiasm.

Jon winced as Belinda raved on about him, the cabin, the barn and, it seemed, everything in it. He laughed to hide his anxiety. "That's enough, partner. I'm sure Miss Burns understands how much you want to stay here with me."

Miss Burns unbent enough to smile. "Yes, I do. And how do you feel about Mrs. Waring, Belinda?"

Jon put a warning hand on B.J.'s. "Miss Burns, I'll have to insist on knowing where you're going with these questions before I allow this to continue. You're obviously alarming Belinda!"

"Frankly, Mr. Waring," the woman said at last as she closed her portfolio. "I'm not at all satisfied that your recent marriage is anything more than an overt attempt to comply with the court's decision."

"I'll be happy to show you our marriage certificate." Jon felt himself on the verge of blowing up and restrained himself with great difficulty. He knew he couldn't afford to lose his temper, too much was at stake here. "I'll even give you the official's name who married us, if that will make any difference."

She waved his offer away. "I can take care of those details myself, but that's not the issue here. In the child's best interests, it's my job to find out if you were actually married to someone who intends to be a wife and a mother to Belinda. Or if this is an attempt to fool the courts. Your possible marriage to a woman you met just a week or two ago is unusual and may not be a healthy setting for an impressionable young girl."

"And what's that supposed to mean?" Jon surged to his feet. He'd been taught that the best defense was a strong offense. If ever there was a time for the latter, it was now. "I hope you're not implying that I would attempt to deceive the court, or something worse. What kind of a place do you think I've got here?"

"Calm yourself, Mr. Waring. I only meant that if this isn't a genuine marriage, your 'wife' may leave at any time once the adoption is approved. That would defeat the purpose of the court's ruling. No," she said firmly, getting to her feet, "to my way of thinking, you and Mrs. Waring hardly know each other, let alone what kind of mother she'd make. It would not only give Belinda the wrong idea of what a real marriage is all about, but there would no longer be a woman's influence to raise her properly if you should part."

Jon was angry. Not only for Belinda's sake, but for Alexandra's. He'd been so focused on the court's dragon lady that he'd forgotten until now that Alex had remained frozen at the door. At Miss Burn's explanation, he saw her face whiten.

No matter how they felt about each other, a protective feeling came over him. He intended to put a stop to Burns making mincemeat out of Alex and their marriage before she got hurt. After all, she'd been blameless in all of this. He'd asked everything of her and, so far, she'd taken nothing for herself. It was up to him to shield her reputation from Burns or anyone else.

It had been why he'd openly introduced her to everyone they'd met, hadn't it?

"I know all I need to know about my wife," he said adamantly, surprised to find he meant every word he was saying. "She's compassionate and loving and, yes, brave. Since you were at the Fourth of July celebration, you may have heard that she saved the lives of B.J. and another kid. A passing stranger wouldn't have been so ready to put her life on the line. No, ma'am! Alexandra may be new to Montana, but she belongs here. At the ranch, and in our lives." He turned his gaze on Alex. "I can personally guarantee she'd going to make a good wife and a mother."

Alex's heart started to melt when she heard his praise. Suddenly she felt ashamed of her anger. She knew enough about him by now to know he wasn't like just any other man, in spite of the words she'd thrown at him. He was hardworking, proud, compassionate, caring. Even behaving like a knight in shining armor, protecting her and her reputation. His biggest crime was trying to be everything to everyone. Including her.

What was happening to her? A short time ago, she'd been ready to tar and feather him. She'd more than half believed he was under the impression his money could buy anything. That he'd used her for his own ends and would say goodbye without a qualm when it came time for her to leave. Now he was laying his thoughts bare; he must care for her.

For the first time since she laid eyes on him, she felt she was seeing the real man. Now that he'd voiced words that were music to her soul, could she leave him?

A tiny flame of growing respect, of hope, grew stronger in her heart as she exchanged looks with Jon. Could she really say goodbye to this man? And to Belinda? A child who had become, in Alex's mind, a young version of herself?

"That's very commendable, I'm sure. But time will tell." Miss Burns stood and gathered her files. "I'm afraid I'm going to have to recommend the approval for the adoption be postponed for a time. If everything is as you say it is, you have nothing to worry about."

"Postponed!" When he saw Alex gasp and heard a tearful cry from B.J., he made a last attempt to reason with Burns. "Come on, surely you don't mean that!"

"Yes, I do. And, I might add, I plan on making occasional visits to the ranch between now and then to make certain everything is as you say it is. I'm truly sorry if this upsets you, Mr. Waring, and you, too, Belinda. But your welfare is my prime concern."

With a hasty goodbye, Letty Burns made her exit.

"You promised everything was going all right, Uncle Jon. It's all your fault," she said, turning on Alex. "I'll never be allowed to stay. I just know it!"

"That's enough, Belinda!" Jon looked down at his angry charge. "It's no one's fault. We'll talk about this later. Right now I want you to go upstairs and get dressed. Alexandra and I have to get dressed, too. Let's all meet in the kitchen later and have breakfast together. Maybe things will look better on a full stomach."

B.J. reluctantly nodded and rushed out of the room.

Alex slowly led the way to the bedroom. She waited until Jon closed the door behind them before she tried to reason with him. "I can't afford to stay here indefinitely. My boss gave me the week off, but he's expecting me back next weekend. Thank goodness it's summer vacation, or I'd miss a whole semester."

"School? You never said anything about going to school."

"I've been taking writing classes at the university during the day and working at the restaurant at night. I simply can't afford to stay here for that length of time. I need the income."

"Don't worry about that," Jon offered. "I'll take care of the financial end of it."

"An offer of another five hundred dollars? What makes you think money solves everything?" Alex was disheartened. All he could think of was the financial end of it. Nothing about his true feelings for her.

She hadn't been wrong about him, after all. He still thought money could buy her. If all he saw was dollar signs when he looked at her, then it was no use. His praise of her had just been another sales job, this time on Miss Burns. "You're already paying me five hundred dollars. That's enough. But it doesn't take care of Miss Burns and the adoption."

"Then what do you suggest I do?"

"Perhaps you should talk to Miss Burns again and try to charm her into filing a positive report." Alex gestured to his nude chest. "And this time with your shirt on."

"You women sure have a thing about shirts, don't you?" He threw the shirt onto the bed. He hadn't intended to hurt or insult her. Didn't she know if she was going to lose her job, it was up to him to help her?

And there was something more. He'd seen the expression on her face when he'd stood up for her to Miss Burns.

It might be the wrong time, but it sure as hell was the right place. His fingers itched to draw her into his embrace, remove her robe and explore her, inch by inch in a field of prairie grass under the sun. And again later, under the stars with evening breezes flowing over their heated bodies. Until she forgot her senseless anger and let him show her what they both wanted.

"I'd rather talk about you and me and where we're headed," he said instead, "but if you want to talk about shirts, it's all right with me."

"Don't be ridiculous. Money and sex. Is that all you think of?" She backed away. "What I really want to do is get dressed and make breakfast. I'm starved."

He picked up the shirt and shrugged it on. "Since it looks as if we're going to be together for a longer time, we'll need to revise the ground rules."

"Your promises, you mean. Promises you can't seem to keep." She glared at him. "You don't really want me around, except for show. No matter what blarney you told Miss Burns. You made that perfectly clear last night when you told me we had to cool it for Belinda's sake."

"Oh, I remember all right. But it's not all Belinda. There's us. Now that the circumstances have changed, it looks as if we're going to have to decide on how we're going to get through the next few weeks."

"There is no us, remember?" she answered bitterly. "Have you forgotten you promised Belinda she would have you to herself? Not that I care. I've always understood I was to leave as soon as her adoption was approved."

"That was then. This is now. No matter how much you might find remaining here with me distasteful, you will stay, won't you?"

"You don't give me much choice, especially since Belinda's adoption seems to depend on it." She looked at him sharply when he made a move in her direction. A determined look was on his face. There was something about this man that got to her, no matter how hard she tried to fight it. She wanted his arms around her, his warm lips caressing hers. And, heaven help her, even when she was angry. "No, I don't want you to touch me. I'll stay as long as I'm needed."

"Good," he said, walking slowly toward her. "Besides, I know you like me."

"And if I do?" Alex asked, backing away. She felt a giant blush cover her from head to toe.

"Just this," he answered as he grabbed her and held her in his arms. He kissed her with a passion that made her knees buckle. With a raised eyebrow, he set her on her feet and grinned over his shoulder as he left the room.

Chapter Eleven

"That's the way it's got to be, Belinda. I mean it. If you want Miss Burns to recommend the adoption papers be approved, you're going to have to play along the way we planned. It's not in your best interests to give Alexandra a hard time."

Jon pushed away his half-filled plate and eyed his sullen ward. "The three of us are going to have to live together until the court agrees to your adoption. We might as well make it easy on each other and act like a family. As far as I can see, we'll never get approved any other way."

"If Stacey was here, Miss Burns would have said yes!" Belinda tossed her head defiantly and glared at him.

"Maybe, maybe not. But she's not here, and Alexandra is." Jon shook his head as he took in Belinda's defiance. "I don't understand what the problem is. All we have to do is behave like a normal family."

The irony of it all was that they *were* behaving like a normal family. And Belinda *was* acting her age. As Alex remembered, almost-twelve was an emotional age, a time when children played a "who's the boss" tug-of-war. Her own father had to set her straight more than once. To add to the problem, Belinda's territorial instincts had come into play.

Alex hid her unease at the argument and rose to clear the table. It was plain to see that Jon didn't know what to make of Belinda. He just didn't remember when he was that age. And, certainly, he had no understanding of a young girl on the brink of becoming a woman.

Belinda resented the fact she and Jon shared the same bedroom, even though she'd suggested it herself only a few days ago. But, Alex realized, that had been before Jon had shown his interest in her.

It wasn't going to be easy for him to strike the right balance between behaving like a father and a friend. Especially when the issue dealt with a stepmother, permanent or not. Jon was doing what he should have done days ago.

And as for Jon, she hoped he understood their truce was going to be a marriage in name only. Though she had her doubts how much longer she could keep up that status if they continued to share the same bed.

For the past three days, she'd been hard put to ignore the question in his eyes as he waited for a sign she was ready to take care of "unfinished business." And after telling her that he thought they should continue their near-platonic relationship because of B.J.! How like a man, she thought as she glanced back to where he was still trying to cajole Belinda into cooperating. Inviting intimacies and at the same time warning her off!

She valued her pride and her sanity too much to give in to those unvoiced questions—even when her senses responded whenever she caught him looking at her with speculation in his eyes.

Last night had been a bear. In the early morning, Jon had stirred, mumbled something in his sleep and reached for her. Before she realized what had happened, he'd moved closer and thrown a muscular leg over her thigh, one hand had reached to cup her breast. When she tried to move away, he had tightened his embrace. Afraid he might awaken, she'd remained frozen in place.

She'd spent the rest of the night sleepless in his arms, burning inside.

That was the last time she'd sleep in the same bed with him, she vowed. It was a question of self-defense. From now on, he could bundle up in the sleeping bag in the easy chair or on the floor. Or, Miss Letty Burns be damned, sleep on the parlor couch. If she had any of the brains left she'd been born with, he would have been sleeping there by now.

THE SOUND OF LAUGHTER drew her to the kitchen window. Jon knelt outside with an armload of new puppies trying to squirm out of his arms and onto the ground. Belinda was pouring a glass of milk into a dish.

"Too bad the litter's mother took off before breakfast," Jon commented as he fished a puppy out of the milk. He picked up the smallest one. "You're going to have to teach this little guy to fend for himself." As if in answer to Jon's comments, the animal jumped onto his shoulder and proceeded to lick his ear. "I guess he's not so helpless, after all," he said, and laughed.

"That's okay, Uncle Jon. I can take care of them all until their mom gets back."

"*If* she comes back." Jon straightened and met Alex's gaze. "Hi, there. Come on out and get some fresh air."

"Soon," she answered. She found herself responding to the good-humored sparkle in his smile, the sight of the puppy sitting on his shoulder. This was more like the Jon she was growing to love, she thought. It was when he was coming on to her that she wanted to run as fast as her feet could take her.

Out of the corner of her eye, she could see Belinda follow Jon's gaze and frown. Her own smile faded. Not much had changed.

She leaned against the window frame and savored the clean, fresh air. Billowing white clouds drifted lazily eastward in a turquoise sky, a gentle breeze whispered through the elm trees shading the cabin. In the distance, she could see verdant grassland, the reflection of water off a meandering stream. The sight fed her soul, eased her aching heart.

At home in Chicago, a long line of automobile traffic would have been slowly making its way along the crowded streets while drivers leaned on their horns in a futile effort to speed things along. On Laurel's main street, friends stopped to chat in front of weather-beaten wooden buildings and horses were still welcome.

Now that she'd experienced the difference, she realized how much she'd grown to appreciate nature's work at its finest and to love the Blue Sky Ranch. And, heaven help her, its virile owner. If only things were different, she could happy be living here with Jon and raising a family. She shook her head. Dreams were for children.

She gazed around the homey kitchen with its vintage appliances. Calico curtains hung at the windows, a large brick fireplace obviously used for cooking and heating when the cabin was built covered one wall. The table and chairs were well-used oak, and the floor a sky-blue linoleum that had been added by an earlier Waring. She thought wistfully of its current owner, a warm, caring and tender man. She envied the lucky woman who would call the cabin and him her own.

She warmed up the coffee and settled down to try to make sense out of her changed life. The past few days living in the same house at arm's length with him had been enlightening. Especially as she began to really know him. He was a loving man, or he wouldn't have wanted to adopt Belinda and befriend her pets. When he'd played with the puppies, she'd seen a side of him that tugged at her heart.

Why couldn't it be like that all the time? And with her?

"Oh, there you are." Jon wandered into the kitchen. "I've been sent to get more milk. By the way, do you need any supplies from town? One of the boys is riding in to pick up some new harnesses I ordered."

"What I need are two strong arms and two willing legs to help out around the house. And a cook. I'm afraid I never learned to cook." She gazed around the kitchen with a sigh. "Do you suppose you can get Anne to come out here to help again?"

Jon was about to tell her he wasn't interested in having her be a housekeeper. That he'd only been teasing when he'd said cooking and cleaning went with nurturing. Until he saw the tired look in her eyes. Now was no time for teasing. "I'll call and ask her to come out to help, but I think what you really need is a day off. How would you like to go river-rafting tomorrow?"

"Is it anything like boating on Lake Michigan?" She poured herself a fresh cup of coffee and one for him. "That's the extent of my experience on water."

"Much better. And, if you don't mind my sounding like a chamber of commerce president, much more scenic. For now," he said as he moved behind her, "how about this?" He placed his hands on her shoulders.

"What are you doing?"

"Massaging your shoulders and neck. You look as if you could use a back rub. How does this feel?"

His strong, muscular hands eased the tension in her shoulders. Then, as thrills of warmth pulsed through her, she realized that he was about to reignite the flame in her heart. Reluctantly she pushed away from the table. The last thing she needed was to let herself get caught back up in his attraction. "Thank you, that felt good. Really, I'm fine. Just a little tired, that's all."

"Then let me show you a part of Montana few people are privileged to see. How about first thing tomorrow morning? I'll ask Rusty to keep an eye on B.J."

"Uncle Jon? You forgot to bring the milk!" A puppy under each arm, Belinda stood in the doorway. Her accusing eyes were fixed on Alex. "The puppies are still hungry!"

Casting a wry glance at Alex, he shrugged, opened the refrigerator door and lifted out a pitcher of milk. As he left the kitchen, he turned back to her. "Tomorrow, then," he said firmly when she shook her head.

THEY WERE DRIFTING along in a raft down the Yellowstone River. Alex enjoyed the serenity and beauty of the waters while Jon pointed out Montana's most striking feature, the rimrocks. The pungent odor of pine trees filled the clear air. Rays of sunshine danced on the water and lit quiet fires of happiness within her. The silence was unbroken except for the sound of the wooden paddles in Jon's hands, dipping into the cold water, and the cry of eagles protesting the invasion of their domain.

Alex put her fears of the future to rest and put everything else out of her mind. She listened to his stories about the river's history and tried to imagine what it must have been like to be a pioneer, seeing these cliffs and grazing meadows for the first time.

The asphalt roads and concrete freeways of Chicago faded from her mind as she leaned back and enjoyed the rocking motion of the raft.

She gazed around her contentedly. "It's so peaceful here, I could almost go to sleep."

"I could change that for you, if you're willing."

"No, thanks. I'm not looking for trouble," she said as she sat back in her seat. Suddenly, at a point where the water broadened to become a wide prairie river with sweeping turns, the motion of the raft accelerated.

Alarmed at the quickened rush of water, her heart began to race. "Jon, we're moving too fast, aren't we?" Before he had a chance to reply, she turned and reached for him. Her sudden movement rocked the raft, and, as she tried to balance herself, she was thrown sideways and fell dangerously close to the edge of the raft.

In a flash, Jon lunged to catch her. His added weight overturned the raft and threw both of them into the water.

The icy rush of water closed over her head. It was so cold, even her teeth ached. The corner of the raft struck her on her right shoulder, and a wave of pain coursed through her. When she gasped in surprise, the water she'd swallowed felt like shards of ice cutting her lungs. She was a strong swimmer, but the shock of falling from the raft disoriented her. Even though she was wearing a life vest, she flailed in the current, trying to grasp onto something solid. Her hands met only rushing water.

What a stupid way to die, she thought as she struggled to swim. She, who daily dodged automobiles on Chicago's busy streets, was going to drown in a river in a remote canyon in Montana, of all places! Damn it, where was Jon when she needed him?

"Hang on, I'm coming!" Stroking hard, Jon finally swam to her side. She slid out of reach. He dived under her and pulled her onto his back. God, she was cold. Well, maybe it didn't matter after all, she thought. All she wanted was to go to sleep. He shouted for her to hang on to his shoulders. It seemed hours before he swam to sandy cover. She felt a tug on her sweater as he clutched her to his chest.

He sank to his knees and lowered her to the sand. Her body was limp, her face gray, almost white. Her closed eyes frightened him. Were they tears or drops of river water that flowed down her cheeks?

"Alexandra! Are you all right?" When she didn't respond, he held her more closely in his arms and wiped the water from her face with a trembling hand. He damned himself for not realizing the river current would change, for bringing her into danger. And for not briefing her on rafting safety rules. He breathed a sigh of relief when he saw her eyelids flutter and a grimace of pain cross her face.

She shuddered in his arms. Whispering words of reassurance, he tried to warm her, rubbed her cold hands and kissed her cold cheeks. Her pale face sent another wave of anxiety through him. When she moaned, he knew he had to do something, and fast.

He laid her on the sand and walked to the river's edge to see if there was a break in the canyon's walls. There were none. They were on a narrow stretch of sandy soil formed by a bend in the river. Pine and poplar trees crowded the lush vegetation, rocks filled the small cove. They were lucky to have capsized at this point—if you could call capsizing lucky, he corrected himself. God alone knows how long they would be marooned in the isolated spot before the raft showed up empty downriver and someone would come looking for them.

He heard Alexandra stir and hurried back to her side. She was coughing and trying to speak.

"Don't try to get up," he said as he gathered her into his arms and wiped the moisture from her face. "You've been hurt, but you're going to be okay. Just relax and let me find out where."

She caught her breath when he ran his hands over her body, kneading, testing her reflexes. Her reflexes were working just fine, she thought fleetingly, too fine. Especially when bursts of electricity shot through her every time the pressure in his hands increased. Her breasts strained against her wet sweater as he fingered her shoulders, her waist, her hips. Wildly she had the strangest desire to throw off her clothing and have his hands slide over her bare skin.

She felt wanton, depraved. How could she think of such things at a time like this? Heaven help her. More drowned than alive, she still wanted him to kiss her, to have his warm breath mingle with hers. To take her then and there, to help her forget everything but this.

"Jon, I..."

"Did I hurt you? I didn't mean to," Jon said anxiously as he checked his hands. "I only wanted to find out if you've been injured."

"I think I hurt my right shoulder, but I'm sure I'll be all right in a minute." She struggled to sit up. "Where are we?"

"Marooned on a small beach. For what it's worth," he said as he looked around at the small cove, "I think we'll be pretty safe here until help arrives."

"I owe you my life, don't I?" Alex struggled to sit up. "It serves me right for not staying on dry land. As much as I've gotten to like Montana, I guess I'm meant for the city." She peered around her. "Chicago was never this dangerous."

Jon damned himself again for exposing her to danger. As strong and game for adventure as she was, the misadventures that had happened to her since she came to Montana were enough to scare off anyone. Let alone a genuine city slicker.

He sighed in resignation and removed what he called his survival belt. In addition to a small folding hatchet, its compartments held assorted items needed for emergencies in the wilderness, items he'd seldom needed until now. He took out a knife and waterproof matches, gathered dry twigs and started a fire. He and Alex had to try to dry out and, too, a fire would guide rescue teams to them. He hung his jacket on a tree limb to dry over the fire, then removed his sodden boots. When his hands went to the buttons on his flannel shirt, Alex stared at him in surprise. "You're not going to take off your clothes, are you? You'll freeze!"

"Just a piece or two."

"Thank goodness for that," she mumbled as she shivered in her wet clothes.

His hands paused in midair. "What did you say?"

"For a minute I thought you were going to..." She blushed as she pictured him bare skinned, his tanned, muscular chest exposed. Fully clothed in damp clothing that left nothing to the imagination, he was breathtaking. Bare...well, it was more than she could afford to think about right now.

Jon eyed her sodden blouse, sweater and jeans. Water continued to drip from her hair, over her face and down her back. She looked cold and miserable. "You need to take some of your clothes off, too. Come on over closer to the fire and get dried out. I don't plan on staying cold and wet if I can help it, and neither should you." He took in the revealing clothing that clung to her like a blueprint. His pulse quickened and his body warmed before his eyes rose to meet hers. From the look on her face, he sensed her thoughts weren't too far from his own.

The wary look on her face made him feel like a fool. She needed something warm, not sexual bantering. "Come on. We can do it in easy stages."

Heat suffused her face. "We'll do *what* in easy stages?"

He eyed her with amusement. "Shame on you. What did you think I had on my mind?" Whatever her answer might have been, she wouldn't have come close to what he was actually thinking. He turned away when his body stirred under his skintight wet jeans. He forced himself to remember this was a crisis and he was, after all, a man sworn to protect her, not to harass her.

"I'm going to check what's back of the bushes. Maybe there's a way out." Fully aware of the change in Jon's body that left nothing to her imagination, Alex scrambled to her feet and made for the bushes at the back of the small beach. Anything to get away from another situation rapidly sliding to the brink of disaster.

She quickly found herself at the back of the small cove littered by bushes and stopped on all sides by a sheer cliff wall. There was no help for it, she had to go back to Jon and temptation. As she hesitated, she felt a pressure on her boot. When she looked down, she saw a long undulating snake slithering over her boots. She closed her eyes and prayed. For a normally intelligent woman, snakes shouldn't have been a problem, but she was feeling pretty stupid right now. Wary eyes on the snake, she backed away and slowly edged her way to the fire—this was no place to hide.

As he added broken pieces of a dead tree branch to the fire, Jon debated going after Alex. No matter how she protested, he intended to bring her back and dry her out as soon as the fire was steady enough to leave.

"Jon, look out!" He looked up to see her scrambling madly over the sand, all the while peering back over her shoulder. He started toward her until he saw her pointing to a large snake slithering along the damp earth toward him. He stopped in his tracks. A quick glance assured him the reptile was harmless, but judging from the fright on Alex's face, it was no time to tease her. He skirted the snake and moved to her side. "Stay put. I can handle this one."

She stared at the snake in horrified disbelief. "Whatever you're going to do," she whispered, "do it now before it's too late."

He picked up a forked tree branch and guided the reptile toward the water. "It's only a king snake on its way back to the riverbank. Actually, it's more frightened of you than you are of it. It won't hurt us.''

"How could I have known it was harmless?" She shuddered. "We don't have snakes in Chicago."

Jon kept a straight face as he took her unresisting body in his arms. When he felt her shiver, he realized there was only one thing to do to get her warm and he didn't intend to wait any longer to do it. Before she could move, he scooped her up into his arms, carried her to the small bonfire and sank down in front of it with her in his arms. "Relax, you'll be fine in a moment."

She smelled of sweet river water and felt so soft, so womanly. He smoothed her damp hair with a gentle hand and placed a comforting kiss on her forehead. Softly, as though she were a child needing comfort, he murmured words of reassurance in her ear.

In seconds, her body reminded him she wasn't a child. He smothered a groan as he looked down at the tempting breasts whose nipples strained against her dripping sweater. Did her hands-off rule apply here, too?

Alex snuggled into his comforting arms. She was where she wanted to be, happy and safe. She murmured her pleasure when he bent his head and kissed her again. This time, she sensed his kiss was different. There was nothing comforting about it. It was more than that. He was a man kissing a woman he wanted. And she was the woman.

He nibbled at her lips and, when she didn't protest, drew her sweater over her head. He reached for the buttons on her shirt. She should make him stop, she thought, until shafts of fire shooting through her body warmed her. When he covered her cold lips with his, she decided she didn't want him to stop. To heck with rules, she thought. They obviously didn't apply in circumstances like this. If today was going to be her last day on earth, she intended to enjoy it.

Droplets of water slid from his curly blond hair to his strong neck and shoulders to disappear beneath his T-shirt as he held her. His broad, rugged chest was outlined in every detail. Even wet, he looked every bit the romantic hero women dreamed of. And he was hers, for now, at least.

She ran her hands over his chest. She wanted to know every inch of him. To feel his firm flesh, to be in his arms. To feel alive.

He pulled away, took off his undershirt and threw it onto the sand close to the fire.

"You'll freeze!"

"Burn, more likely," he answered. Holding her with a fiery gaze, he dropped to her side and gathered her into his arms again.

"Alexandra?"

"Yes," she whispered, running her hands over his shoulders and down his arms. His tongue touched her breasts with fire. His fingers pressed into her back as he held her to him and moved his body against her. The friction of his now-heated skin against hers sent her past the point of no return.

She heard him sigh. "Something wrong?"

"Yes, this." He bent to the task of removing her shirt and bra. She shivered in his arms. "You'll be warm in a minute," he said with a soft smile. "And that's another promise."

She caressed the rugged length of him, tongued his nipples, the hollow beneath his throat. Pleasure stung her fingers. Wanting him as much as he wanted her, she pressed closer still, felt his arousal against her thigh.

"I don't know how much of this I can take," he gasped when her hands moved lower. "Let me know when you're finished exploring."

When her hands continued to move over him, he grasped her by her shoulders and turned her beneath him. "On the other hand," he growled, "we can always explore together later on. Right now, there's something more important going on."

Her heart missed a beat when he laid her on his warm shirt, drew off her jeans and with his knee urged her legs apart. When he joined his body with hers, it seemed to be with infinite care. Testing her need, betraying his own. He moved slowly, deliberately building her desire until she wanted to beg for something just out of her reach. He seemed to understand. He smiled and whispered, "This one is for you, the next one will be for both of us."

She could feel the sand under the shirt against her sensitive skin. His rough hands sliding down her thighs aroused her even more. She was burning, sliding closer and closer to the fire. Behind her closed eyes, the heavens shattered into a thousand pieces. She touched the fire and exploded into wild, exquisite sensations.

He bent and kissed her lips, his movements accelerated. With a cry of completion, he fell to her side murmuring her name.

Good Lord, she thought as reason slowly returned. Nothing had prepared her for this storm of pleasure. She'd given in to an overwhelming need for this man, and she still wanted more.

Her heart beat wildly as she fought for control. All her senses cried for still more of the taste of him, the hot sweet touch of lips and tongue, for the arms that had crushed her. Of being taken where reason had no place.

Her body felt warm and welcoming as she nodded sleepily and snuggled closer. He wanted more of her, too.

"Jon? What did you call this?"

"Exploring," he said with a fond laugh as he kissed her forehead. "I thought you were sleeping."

In a voice thick with passion, she replied, "Do you suppose we could get on with the one for both of us?"

"You bet." As he bent to kiss her lovely lips, he threw all thoughts of their predicament aside. He was certain rescue would come eventually, but not, he hoped, too soon. These moments with Alexandra in his arms were all that mattered.

Soon Alex, partially dressed, was asleep in his arms. Warmed by the fire and by the aftermath of an afternoon of lovemaking, he closed his own eyes and reviewed the past few weeks.

Marriage to Alexandra was much more than he'd contemplated when they'd been confronted with the facts—they were man and wife on paper. And now, they were man and wife in truth. What would she say and do when she realized that danger had pushed them over the edge? As far as he was concerned, he was willing to pay the piper. Happiness was in his arms.

The faint sound of a motor sounded in the distance. He could see spotlights searching the shoreline. "Wake up, sleepyhead. It looks as if we're about to be rescued."

"Oh, my God!" Alex scrambled to her feet and reached for her sweater. "Quick, hand me my sweater. I wouldn't want anyone to know something was going on here."

Jon had to admire the speed with which Alex put herself together. Most women would have become hysterical over an ordeal like the one she'd just been through. If ever a woman was meant to belong to him, he decided, it was she.

"Well, Jon. Looks as if you and your new missus are right cozy, fire and all." As Jon helped him beach the boat, a laughing ranger took in Alex's struggle to get into her damp sweater. His eyes swung to Jon's unbuttoned shirt. "Sure you want to be rescued?"

Chapter Twelve

"Well, boss, it's right good to see you and your missus safe and sound," the ranch cook said, pumping
Jon's hand vigorously. A broad smile lit up his
weather-beaten face. "When the ranger called and told
me what happened, I grabbed a few blankets and
hightailed it up here. From what he said, it sure
sounded like it was a close call."

"Too close for comfort," Jon agreed, anxious eyes
on his bedraggled and forlorn wife. "Guess a couple
of the boys will have to go on up to the raft landing
and bring back my Jeep. Right now, let's get on our
way. We need to get out of these wet clothes."

He'd downplayed their danger for her sake, but the
truth was they'd come closer to tragedy than he liked
to think. The thought of losing her so soon after realizing how much she meant to him hit him square in
his gut. Doubtful of her ability to cope when he'd first
seen her in her pink silk suit, he'd unexpectedly found
her to be a woman he could depend on.

She was a woman he could see himself spending his
life with.

Except, there was still B.J. to consider.

Grateful for Alex's silence on the way back to the ranch, he mused over the way his life had changed since she'd come into it. His grandfather had once told him life was like a turning wagon wheel, each spoke another day, a new opportunity. Granddad had been right, only Jon's wagon wheel was turning faster than he could handle.

The air had gotten noticeably cooler with the setting sun. Still wearing damp clothes, Alex shivered under the blanket the genial ranch cook had brought with him. "How long before we get home?" she asked, her teeth chattering. "I can't wait to get into a hot shower. I'm not only cold, I'm starving. In fact, I've never felt so miserable in my whole life."

"Soon." Jon comforted her as he gazed at the darkening sky. "Looks as if we'll just make it back in time before the rain starts." He welcomed the rain as long as it held off until he had Alexandra tucked warmly in bed, with him beside her.

"Rain?" She looked up through the open top of the Jeep at the darkening sky. "I've had enough water to last me a lifetime. Where's all that sunshine we had this morning?"

"Sorry. Summer storms come up pretty fast around here, and often. That's what keeps Montana green year-round. Don't worry, we'll get back before it starts."

He positioned his body around her to give her added warmth and rubbed her cold fingers. The realization of how close they'd come to catastrophe still scared the hell out of him. He was a strong swimmer, thank God, for she'd been too stunned to save herself. They'd been luckier than she knew. If the threatening rain had come earlier and caused the river to rise, the small strip of sand and dirt on which they'd been stranded would have been underwater. There would have been no dry tree branches to make a bonfire and nowhere to wait for rescue except for the treetops. If they were lucky.

"Feel a little warmer?" he murmured against her pale cheek. When she nodded, he playfully fingered her damp hair. "I should have done a better job at the ranger station of getting you dry. I promise," he added with a wicked grin, trying to get her mind off her discomfiture, "it'll be the first thing I do when we get home."

"After a hot shower, I hope?" Her eyes extended an invitation that held him enthralled.

"Maybe, even during a hot shower." He caressed the nape of her neck and, pleased when she relaxed against him, kissed the lush lips that tantalized him so.

Alex forgot their differences as she settled contentedly into his sheltering arms, as they were nothing compared to what she and Jon had been through. The warmth of his lips sliding against hers sent welcome sparks shooting through her. At her soft moan of pleasure, she saw his eyes glint, felt him kiss her with a new urgency. If possible, she was more taken with him than ever.

Jon's strength and quick reaction had saved her from drowning. Now she felt herself drowning in his compelling eyes. How circumstances change, she thought as a wave of anticipation shot through her.

The interlude on the damp sands of the cove hadn't been enough. She wanted much more of him.

When Cookie drove the ranch Jeep up to the cabin porch, Jon could see a BMW rental car parked at its side. A number of suitcases stood waiting outside the door.

He had a sinking feeling. That damn wagon wheel was turning up more trouble than it already had. "Thanks, Cookie. I owe you one." Jon surveyed the quiet surroundings. The yard and its surroundings were empty. The silence was broken only by animal sounds coming from the barn. "Rusty and B.J. and the boys still gone?"

"Yeah. Good thing I came back after nooning. I was the only one left around to take the call from the ranger station. I expect the men will be back anytime now." Cookie followed Jon's gaze to the porch. "Looks like you've got company come to stay, boss."

"Lord, I hope not," Jon said under his breath as he helped Alex out of the Jeep. From the way his sixth sense was quivering like a string on an electric guitar, he had a sinking feeling he was about to encounter the last person in the world he wanted to meet. He glanced over at Alex and fleetingly wondered what her reaction would be to their unwelcome visitor when they met. Not much better than his, probably. "Company's the last thing we need right now."

"Dunno." The wiry older man scratched the stubble of a gray beard on his face. "I'd say maybe you've got more than one visitor from all that baggage. And from the looks of it, they plan on staying for a long time. You know, boss, it's a good thing I'd already put a big stew on to simmer before I went to get you."

"Cookie," Alex said, distracted from the sight of the suitcases by the mention of food, "if you have anything fit to eat, please lead me to it. I'm so hungry I could even tackle one of those beefalo burgers Jon's always talking about."

"Well, shoot, Mrs. Waring," he apologized, "I wish I'd known you like beefalo. I can't oblige this time, but if you got your heart set on it, I'll try to round you up a nice big beefalo steak tomorrow."

"I was only joking," Alex hastily reassured the crestfallen cook. "I'm more than happy to take anything you have."

"Go along to the house, missus. I'll bring up a pan of stew in a few minutes. Got a few leftover biscuits, too." He set off for the cook house at double speed.

"Alexandra..." Jon decided to bite the bullet before it shot him in the foot. "I have something to say you may not want to hear. I'm afraid we've got company."

She glanced at the stack of suitcases on the porch. "I thought as much, but I was so busy thinking about how cold and hungry I am, I couldn't think of anything else. Were you expecting someone?"

"No, but I've the feeling she's here, anyway."

"She?" Alex stopped in her tracks. She suspected, even as she didn't want to hear him confirm her suspicions, who was here. And from the funereal tone in Jon's voice, she felt his visitor wasn't going to be welcomed. She didn't blame him. Things were complicated enough already. She glanced down at the sorry state of her clothes and wished she looked less like a drowned rat. "Is 'she' who I think she is?"

Jon shrugged his shoulders. "It looks as if Stacey's decided to come home."

"Yes, I suppose it does." Alex solemnly studied the large number of suitcases. "And it certainly looks as if she's planning to stay awhile."

"'Fraid so," Jon kicked a rock out of his way and cursed under his breath when he felt pain shoot up his big toe. The prospect of having Stacey finally here left him cold. They would have all been better off if she had remained six thousand miles away.

He gazed down at the concern written on Alex's face. She deserved more than the unforeseen things that had been happening to her.

Just when he'd thought things were going to be okay between them, they were confronted with a new complication. Meeting Stacey, he knew from the way his luck was going, wasn't going to be easy for any of them. "I guess we might as well go on in and face our guest."

"Her timing is certainly off, isn't it?" Alex gazed uneasily at the suitcases. "I'm afraid to think of what's going to happen when Miss Burns finds out Stacey's here."

"Nothing, if I can help it," Jon said firmly. He took her by the arm and led her up the steps. "As far as I can see, Burns believed me when I told her Stacey and I broke up before I married you. Unless someone talks, Burns shouldn't question her appearance. After all, Stacey and I have known each other all our lives. It shouldn't seem out of the ordinary for her to visit."

"For a visit? Just like a man." Alex laughed as she pictured Miss Burns's reaction at finding Stacey in residence at the ranch. "Personally, I don't think Miss Burns would swallow that explanation. She might wonder why Stacey would come here after you told her you and I had gotten married. An extra woman on a honeymoon doesn't make much sense. You'll have to think of a better reason than that."

"Well . . ." Jon hesitated and avoided meeting her eyes. "The truth is, I didn't exactly tell Stacey the whole story."

"You didn't *exactly* tell her?" Alex came to a stop and swung on Jon. "What *did* you tell her?"

"Fact is, I couldn't reach her the second time I called to tell her you and I had actually gotten married by mistake. I just left a message thinking someone would eventually give it to her. I sure hope they did," he muttered under his breath as he held the screen door aside for Alex to enter, "or we're in for a hell of a lot of trouble."

"You hope!" Alex clutched the blanket under her chin more tightly and gazed cautiously at the suitcases. "And what are you going to do if no one was able to deliver your message?"

Her question was answered when a barefoot, tall, willowy blonde in a crimson sundress came sailing out the downstairs bedroom door with a wide smile on her face.

"Jonnie, I'm here!"

"So I see," he said, unsuccessfully dodging the arms she was trying to throw around his neck. He cast a helpless look at Alexandra over Stacey's shoulder. "You could have called to let me know you were coming."

"Oh that! I was moving in such a hurry I didn't have time to stop to call. I thought you would be glad to see me," Stacey said, surprised when he moved out of reach. "After all, we did have an understanding." She noticed the blanket-clad Alex standing silently behind Jon. "And who is this?"

Jon hesitated, took a deep breath and drew Alex to his side. "You're not going to be happy to hear this, but I'd like you to meet my wife, Alexandra Storm Waring."

"Don't be ridiculous, Jonnie." Stacey smiled archly at him. "This is no time to tease me. Don't tell me you've already forgotten I'm the woman you married?" The look on his face sent warning signals shooting through her. "Now that I'm here, you don't have to keep up the pretense any longer." Puzzled at his reaction, she studied his solemn face for a minute before she looked over Alex.

"Are you the proxy bride?" When Alex nodded, Stacey added brightly. "Thank you so much for helping us out, but you won't be needed any longer now that I've come home."

Alex felt as if a giant hand were squeezing her heart. The day had started with an angry goodbye from Belinda, gone on to see her miss drowning by a miracle, giving herself to Jon and now this. Without a doubt, this might turn out to be the worst day of her life. She straightened to her full height, held the blanket around her more tightly and shot a cold glance at Jon. "I'll leave you to do the explaining. Right now, I need a hot shower. I'll catch up with you later." Before he could stop her, she headed for the bedroom.

"Jonnie? What does she mean by that?" Stacey asked, gazing after Alex. "What explaining?"

Alex could hear Stacey's surprised questions behind her as she fled down the hall and to the bedroom. A purse and an open overnight case lay on the bed, black patent leather shoes had been thrown haphazardly on the rug. With a lump in her throat that threatened to choke her, she gathered fresh clothing from the dresser drawer and headed for the bathroom and a hot shower. Whatever Stacey had in mind by coming to the Blue Sky Ranch was obvious.

She'd come home to be Jon's wife.

"COME ON IN THE KITCHEN with me while I put on some coffee. I'm frozen. I could use a pot of it while I thaw out," Jon said as he watched Alex disappear from sight. He was going to have to postpone that dual shower he'd been planning. And, from the look on Alex's face, he had a rotten feeling he might not be able to take it anytime soon.

"We've got a lot to talk about, Stace. I've got a hunch we're both going to need something strong before I get through explaining what's happened." Brushing aside her questions, Jon led the way to the kitchen.

"You might want to sit down while I tell you the whole story. But before I do..." He paused and listened for the sound of the shower water running. He didn't know how well this conversation would go, but the last thing he wanted was for Alex to be hurt by something Stacey might say.

"What is there to talk about? I came back to be your wife."

Jon turned off the stove, reached for a cup and poured coffee. "Wait here a minute, I'll be right back."

He carried a cup of steaming black coffee to the bathroom door. Satisfied by the sound of running water and the sound of her singing that Alex was still in the shower, he cautiously opened the door. Through the sheer shower curtain, he could see her bending over and washing her hair. Although the steam formed a fleecy white cloud around her, he had no difficulty picturing every delectable detail of Alex's body. He had no difficulty remembering how much they'd enjoyed each other on a blanket spread on damp sand.

He would have given a lot to be able to join her in the shower, reassure her that she belonged to him and had no intention of letting her go. But Stacey was waiting. He gazed at Alex's silhouette for a wishful moment before he saw her reach to turn off the water. He had to get out of here, fast, or he wouldn't be able to leave. He put the cup on the sink where she would find it, and, before she had a chance to notice him, he hurried back to the kitchen where Stacey was waiting for him.

"What I'm trying to tell you, Stace—" he took a deep breath and plunged in " —is after I got the faxed copy of the marriage application with your signature agreeing to a proxy wedding ceremony, I advertised for a woman to stand in for you. Alexandra answered the ad." At her reluctant nod, he went on to recount the story of the botched wedding ceremony and how Potter had inadvertently performed a real marriage. "We tried to get out of it, but, bottom line, Alexandra *is* my wife."

Stacey couldn't believe what she was hearing. "There must be some mistake! I told you I would be back someday! That should have counted for something," she said in her defense, surprised when he appeared to be more troubled than ever. "After all, didn't I agree to be your wife when you asked me to help you?"

"Yes, you did, and I'm grateful. But *someday* wasn't good enough, Stace. I had to do something fast to satisfy the court or they wouldn't let me adopt B.J. Besides, since you were only doing it as a favor, I didn't dream you'd take it this way.

"Coffee, Stace?" He poured her a cup of coffee, took one for himself and joined her at the table. The apprehensive look in her eyes tore him in two. She meant a lot to him. After all, they'd been engaged at one time and were still good friends. He could tell she was troubled, that what he had to say was going to hurt her. But his own story couldn't wait, especially since it seemed to affect her as much as it affected him.

He tried his coffee and grimaced. "Too hot and too strong, isn't it?" He swallowed hard. "Fact is, when I advised the court you and I were going to get married I had no idea they would send someone to check me out. I found it out after the marriage ceremony when I called home. It was shortly after that I found out from the county marriage clerk Alexandra and I were really married. I couldn't reach you, so I left a message for you. I had no choice but to ask her to come back here."

"Surely you knew I would be back! I've always kept my word with you." Stacey was stunned. Jon had been her only hope. Without him, she was in more trouble than she could have possibly anticipated. As it was turning out, her expectations crumbled into dust. It took all of her willpower to focus on what he was telling her.

"No, I didn't. And not in time. Not from what you were telling me on the telephone, anyway. Something about a special reason why you had to stay in Europe, wasn't it? You loved a guy named Faoud, remember?"

"Yes, I remember." Unbidden tears came into her eyes before she had a chance to catch herself. "I still do. But our relationship is hopeless. Even though we love each other, Faoud and I come from two different worlds, two different cultures. And they're not exactly compatible. As a matter of fact, I had to come home before he got himself killed over me. Or before I was the one who got killed."

Jon handed her a towel and watched sympathetically while she dried her eyes. "Gosh, I'm sorry, Stace. It sounds like a real horror story. Surely, it can't be as bad as all that."

"It is," she cried. "And although it's hard to believe, worse."

"Then I guess you're obviously in a heck of lot more trouble than I am." He covered her trembling hands with his. "Almost like when we were kids growing up together, eh, Stace?"

"What we had then was a piece of cake," she murmured into the towel. "Children don't get into this kind of trouble. It's not like when you rescued me from a tree."

"It can't be all that bad, Stace. After all, you've fallen in love with a man you just met. Maybe you can fall out just as easily."

As he spoke, Jon thought about his relationship with Alexandra. He hadn't realized how deeply he'd fallen in love with her, how much she meant to him. Not until today when he'd almost lost her. He faced the fact squarely: he did love her and he didn't intend to lose her. Falling in love hadn't come easily, not when he'd had no interest in marriage. And as if that hadn't been difficult enough, falling out of love with her seemed impossible.

"Sorry. That was an asinine statement coming from a guy like me, wasn't it? Especially after what you and I went through together." He rubbed her cold hands. "I guess we still do care about each other, at that. I never planned it this way. And I certainly never meant to hurt you. You've been too good a friend."

"Thank you for that." Stacey glanced at the door before she continued. She hated to plead with him, except there was so much at stake. "Since your marriage to Alexandra is only on paper, maybe you can get it annulled quietly?"

Stacey's question brought Jon out of his chair. An annulment? He didn't know how to answer her, couldn't even meet her hopeful eyes. He remembered a time in college when they were young and thought they were in love. Then they'd become engaged and planned to marry. Their plans had been canceled after graduation, when she'd told him she wanted a big career and he had the ranch to run.

Even after they'd broken up, they'd remained best friends. Stacey was a trusted friend whom he had asked to help in his proxy marriage scheme, even if she hadn't come through at the end. He owed her for old times' sake and for even more, for inadvertently making it possible for him to find Alexandra.

"I'm sorry, Stace, but an annulment is impossible. In fact, I don't even know why you'd care." He felt like all kinds of a fool as he remembered lovemaking in the sand. Embarrassed, he finally told her the truth. "My marriage to Alexandra is more than on paper."

"Oh, no!" She stared at him, lowered her head and broke into wrenching sobs. Her only hope was gone. "I never expected this could happen. You and I have always steered clear of marriage before. I never dreamed you'd wind up married now. I don't know what I'm going to do."

Shocked, Jon came around the table and lifted her into his arms. "Don't cry, Stace. Whatever the problem is, it can't be *that* bad."

"It is!" she cried. "It's a matter of life and death. I have to get married before it's too late!"

"Good Lord, what do you mean by that?" Jon was shaken to the core by her outburst. "Whose life and death?"

"Mine and Faoud's, and the baby's."

"What baby?"

"I'm expecting a baby." She gazed at him through tearful eyes. "Oh, don't tell me single women have children all the time. I'm aware of that. It's not the reason I have to get married."

"Come on in the other room with me where we can talk without anyone hearing us." His heart ached for her as he dried her eyes. "We'll have more privacy there and you can tell me the whole story."

He felt like a heel knowing it wasn't only privacy he wanted; he didn't want to chance Alex hearing Stacey's story. His marriage didn't need any more problems. "Here, sit down and take a deep breath. There's something more to this than a pregnancy, isn't there? You can tell me. Remember how we used to bend each other's ear about everything when we were growing up? Especially when we were in trouble. Tell me what's going on."

Stacey hesitated. She'd come this far, she'd have to go the rest of the way. Her only hope was to persuade Jon to help her somehow, even without marriage. "Promise you won't tell anyone?"

"I promise."

"Not even Alexandra?"

"Especially not Alexandra."

She took a deep breath. She had to tell someone, and who better than someone she'd known and trusted all her life? "Faoud is a political figure from somewhere in the Middle East. I'm not going to tell you where, it's too dangerous for you to know. Anyway, we were at an international news conference several months ago and fell in love the first time we met. Later when I told him about the baby we decided to get married. But his advisor told him his people and his family would never permit him to be seen with me because of cultural differences, let alone understand if they knew we were lovers. We had to meet secretly.

"If it comes out we were together," she went on to say, "and that he's the father of my child, I'm afraid they'd kill me. And my baby. He sent me home to you when I told him about our proxy marriage arrangement and advised me to tell you the truth. And that he'd figure out something later."

"So that's why you came home," Jon said haltingly. Things were far more complicated than he'd realized. "To have a father for the baby?"

"Yes. I was going to tell you about it later." She shrugged her shoulders helplessly. "I confess I was counting on you to help me. Since it was going to be a marriage only of convenience, I didn't think you'd mind. Now that you've gotten married, I don't know what to do."

Jon rose and paced the floor. The tears in her eyes and the sorrow in her voice tore at his heart. She meant a lot to him, always had. But Alexandra meant so much more. Still, he couldn't abandon Stacey. Not at a time like this.

"That's a tough one, all right. I've already introduced Alexandra as my wife to everyone, including Letty Burns, the caseworker from the court. She came and checked us out, but I'm not sure we fooled her. B.J.'s adoption hasn't been approved yet and it won't be until after she comes back again to check on us. I have to be very circumspect until then. And besides, I don't know how I can switch wives now. The court would never understand, let alone the half of Montana that seems to know Alex and I are married. I might even lose the chance to adopt B.J."

"I'm sorry to have made such a mess of things, Jonnie. In the beginning, I never realized how opposed Faoud's people could be to someone like me. When it became clear that it might be a matter of life or death, I had to come home. I have the baby to consider. You were my only hope." Tears came back into her eyes as she realized she'd come back too late. She'd prayed that Jon could help her. If not Jon, who could? "You're right, Jonnie. We *are* both in trouble."

"We'll think of something, Stace." He held her in his arms as he tried to comfort her. "I promise everything will turn out all right."

Touched by Jon's thoughtfulness when she'd found the cup of steaming coffee waiting for her, Alex was on her way to tell him so. Convinced Jon cared for her as a husband should care for a wife, she'd thought the problem of Stacey's return to claim him for her own husband would be settled by now. She stopped when she heard Jon and Stacey talking as she came down the hall.

Her mother had always told her an eavesdropper never heard any good things about himself. Smiling at the memory, she started to turn back. She caught her breath as she heard Stacey mention a baby and that marriage to Jon was her only hope. Through the thunder that exploded in her ears, she heard Jon actually mention the prospect of switching wives.

Blindly she made for the bedroom. Her first instincts as to the reason Jon and Stacey wanted to get married in a proxy ceremony had been correct. B.J.'s adoption hadn't been his only motive. In spite of his skirting the issue when she'd first confronted him with her suspicion, he *was* the father of Stacey's baby!

Chapter Thirteen

If it hadn't brought back so many memories, Alex reflected grimly as she made plans to leave, she would have left wearing her pink silk suit. But she couldn't bring herself to put it on. Not when it reminded her of so much. Of answering an advertisement for a proxy bride, of a botched wedding ceremony that had made her a real bride, and of incredible lovemaking that had turned her into a wife in more than name.

Just getting involved in a proxy marriage in the first place made her question her sanity. Except that once she'd gotten over her stage fright and had taken a good look at the groom, she'd had the overwhelming desire to fantasize she was his wife—if only for the duration of the ceremony. When the justice of the peace had told the groom he could kiss his bride, she remembered instinctively responding as if she had really been his bride.

The groom had been tall, ruggedly handsome with intelligent eyes. He'd stirred her in a way she hadn't understood back then, but she understood it now. Her senses had spoken to her, and she'd answered their call.

She pictured him again in his Western wedding finery. A strong, masculine man of the West, with an unconscious air of sensuality about him that had made her senses tumble over themselves. His expressive green eyes haunted her. His lips had kissed her in a way a woman dreamed of being kissed. She'd been as surprised as he at the intensity of the way she'd returned the kiss. But, lost in her fantasy, she hadn't been able to help herself.

And now, although she'd known him for only two short weeks, she couldn't imagine a life without being cradled in his arms, kissed with firm lips that drew the last ounce of carnal response from her.

It was more than his looks or his air of sensuality that still drew her, she realized. He was a strong, responsible man; thoughtful, kind and caring. A natural leader, he had the respect and admiration of all the townspeople of Laurel, who had even made him their honorary mayor and president of the chamber of commerce.

He was a rare man, who thought of others before he thought of himself.

Belinda and Stacey were lucky to have him.

Tears came to her eyes as she blindly searched for fresh clothing. She wished she'd never met him, had never shared such ecstasy in his arms. She would never forget him, never stop wanting him, but it was no use torturing herself. He clearly belonged to someone else, and that someone was here.

She glanced at the clothing through tear-filled eyes. There was no choice at all: the pink suit or the things Jon had purchased for her in Laurel. She hurriedly dressed in jeans, a cotton blouse and the brown leather cowboy boots. She'd mail them back to him when she got home, or give them to the Goodwill.

The frivolous silk suit and matching shoes she'd worn the day of her wedding were crammed into her overnight case. About to reach for the sheer, short nightgown she'd brought with her a lifetime ago, she tossed it aside. There were too many memories in its silken threads.

"Alexandra? May I come in?"

She froze at the sound of his voice before she realized he had no way of knowing she'd overheard him talking to Stacey. No clue to how hurt she felt knowing he'd lied to her from the beginning of their relationship. Or that she knew he was the father of Stacey's child. Her pride and everything they'd shared together wouldn't allow her to confront him with her knowledge.

She loved him too much to hurt him. If their relationship had to end, she intended to end it without anger or recriminations. And, because she wanted to spare them both any further heartache, she intended to be the one to walk away.

"Alexandra?"

She forced a smile and threw open the door. "Come on in. I was just going to find you."

Jon saw her overnight case at her feet and her purse in her hands. His eyebrows rose at the crumpled sheer nightgown lying at the foot of the bed. "Where are you going?"

"To find Cookie and ask him to take me into town," she said, masking her aching heart by casually checking her watch and looking in her purse for her airplane ticket. "I'll catch a bus to the Billings airport from there."

"Just because he didn't have a beefalo steak handy?" he joked as he reached for her. "Do we have a problem?" he asked cautiously when she dodged his hands.

"Not anymore," she answered, although her smoky eyes told him something else. "At least, I don't," she said. "You might when Miss Burns shows up. But," she added through a throat suddenly choked with pain, "you're great at storytelling. I'm sure you'll be able to think up something good."

"And what is that supposed to mean?" Jon was shocked at the change in her. The last time he'd seen her was behind a shower curtain singing happily. "Are you sure you feel all right?" he asked, hoping he could settle whatever was bothering her tonight. He took another tentative step toward her.

"Don't touch me!" She backed away as if she were afraid of him.

"Don't touch you?" Jon felt as though he'd run smack into a brick wall that was about to tumble down on him. It was that damn wheel spoke again, he thought with despair, bringing with it a day that was rapidly going downhill, headed for disaster. And taking him with it. "Come on, sweetheart," he coaxed as he inched toward her. "Tell me what's wrong. You know we've been wanting to touch each other all day long. That, and a heck of a lot more."

"I've changed my mind," she said, glancing down at her overnight bag then over his shoulder as if gauging the distance to the door.

"A promise is a promise," he said, trying to make light of a situation that was making his head spin. "Since you've already taken your shower, give me a few minutes to take mine and I'll deliver on that promise."

"Oh no, you won't," she stormed, forgetting her intention to leave quietly and like a lady. Martyrdom be damned! "I need more of that nonsense like I need a hole in the head. In fact, I don't need you at all. Apparently, Stacey is the one who needs you!"

"Whoa, there! Where did that come from?" Shaken, he felt his heart skip a beat, a feeling of dread come over him. He watched her pull the wedding ring off her finger and thrust it out to him to take. "No, thanks." He put his hands in his still-damp pockets to keep from shaking the truth out of her. "You might as well get everything off your chest. Is there something you're trying to tell me?"

"It should be pretty clear by now. I intend to leave. Here, take this, I don't need it anymore." She tried once more to give him the ring.

"No way!" He pushed her hand away, his frustration boiling to the surface. They'd come so close to understanding each other, so close to making a marriage based on mutual respect and trust. And, yes, even love. Lord only knows how much he'd grown to love her. He didn't intend to have their marriage end this way. Not until she told him what was wrong, and maybe not even then.

"You're not going anywhere until you tell me what's bothering you. If you have something sensible to say, spit it out and we'll try to settle the problem like two sensible people. If not, supper's waiting. Cookie delivered a big pot of stew and biscuits to go with it."

"I'll be sure and thank him later, but right now I'm anxious to get on my way." She picked up her overnight case and started for the door. "You can keep the rest of the things you bought for me. I won't need them in Chicago."

Jon stalked to the door ahead of her and turned the key. "You're not leaving," he repeated firmly, his eyes locking with hers as he dropped the key into his back pocket.

"You can't keep me here!"

"Try me." His set expression dared her to try. "You're not going to Chicago or anywhere else. I waited thirty-five years to get married and I don't intend to have it end like this. Certainly not until I know what has you riled up all of a sudden."

"It's actually very simple, now that I know the whole truth behind the proxy marriage. You never intended to get married, really married, at least to me. It was all a big mistake, and now you can rectify it," she rejoined as she gestured to the bed. "With me gone, maybe you can get on with a real marriage."

"A real marriage," he echoed thoughtfully as he gazed at her. Alexandra's tightly set mouth and hazel eyes glistening with unshed tears spoke of something more than anger. Sadness radiated from every part of her body. He followed her gesture to the bed, looking for clues. His questions were answered when he saw Stacey's initialed overnight bag and purse flung on the bed covers. Light finally dawned. His racing heart settled down to a normal beat.

"Good Lord, you're jealous of Stacey!"

"I suppose you would say so. I call it facing the truth." Alex couldn't meet his eyes for fear she would break down in front of him. Her every heartbeat was a beating drum sounding the end of the fairy-tale marriage and her fantasy lover. She drew a deep breath when his eyes darkened. No matter what had been his motive for the marriage, she was certain he hadn't intended to hurt her. Even if he hadn't played fair with her, she felt she owed him some kind of an explanation. "Actually, it's more than just Stacey. It's yours and Stacey's baby I had in mind."

"My baby?" He ran his hands over his forehead in frustration and paced the room. "Now, I've heard everything!" He paused in midstride and glared at her. "First it's Stacey, and now a baby! I don't know where you got that fool idea. If you're talking about B.J., she's more woman than child, as you've so carefully pointed out."

"All right, let's be completely honest with each other." Alex threw her bag on the bed, placed her hands on her hips and glared back at him. If he wanted the truth, she'd give it to him. "You might as well know I overheard you and Stacey talking about her pregnancy. And that she's come back here so that the child would have its father. You."

Jon relaxed. That damned wagon wheel spoke had started to move again, thank God. Now that he understood what he was dealing with, he had another chance. He eyed his spitfire wife. He knew how to handle anger, it was unexplained sadness he had trouble with.

He wanted to hold her in his arms and kiss and comfort her until she calmed down. To explain, to show her how much she meant to him. And to proceed with an armistice. But she looked too determined and too angry for that kind of bloodless warfare.

"Alexandra," he said as he moved carefully toward her, "from what you've told me, I gather you didn't hear all of our conversation?"

"Maybe not, but I heard enough." She backed away as he came closer. "I had no intention of eavesdropping. I just wanted to come and thank you for the hot coffee I found waiting for me after I came out of the shower."

"I thought so." He grasped her cold hand before she could snatch it away, and led her to the easy chair. "Sit," he said. She remained standing, defying him, her eyes still blazing with an emotion akin to outrage. He knew he had to alter his approach or he wasn't going to get anywhere with her. "Please?" When she finally relented and sank into the chair, he knelt in front of her and took her hands in his.

"Look at me, sweetheart," he said tenderly. "If you had listened to the rest of our conversation, yes, you would have heard Stacey mention she had to get married because she's pregnant. But you also would have heard that some other man is the father of her child, not me."

Good, he thought. At least she was listening to what he was saying. "I can't tell you much more than that, I promised to keep the man's identity a secret. In fact, I wasn't going to tell you about the baby at all until you mentioned it. From what Stacey told me, there are reasons she and the baby's father can't get married. And that she's in some kind of danger. That's why she has to appear to have a father for her child."

"And that's where you come in?"

"Yes. I'll be honest with you. She *did* come back believing she and I were married—just as we'd planned when I first called and asked her to help me with B.J.'s adoption. She was hoping our proxy marriage would make it appear I was the baby's father. It was the only way she could avoid terrible consequences if the truth were known. It seems she never got the message I left for her at her hotel when it turned out you and I were actually married."

"Did she have reason to believe you would become her true husband?" Some of her sadness seemed to disappear as he explained Stacey's problem, but her eyes were wary.

"Only on paper. We had always intended to get the marriage annulled sometime in the future after the adoption went through. We both know whatever she and I had between us years ago is over, but we've remained good friends. But, right now, Stacey needs a front, a husband, desperately. At least until her lover comes for her." *If he ever does.*

Alex held her breath as his explanation sank in. From all she'd seen and heard, Stacey did have reason to believe Jon would be willing to pretend to be the husband she needed so desperately. The flicker of hope that his first few words had started to kindle threatened to turn into ashes when she realized how desperate Stacey's situation was. "And do you intend to become that husband once you get rid of me?"

"How could you even think it?" He unfurled her clenched left hand, kissed her fingers, one by one, and put the discarded rings back on her finger. "No matter what I intended when I advertised for a proxy wife, I promised Potter I would take you for better or for worse. Even if I have broken a few of the other promises I made, I intend to keep that one." The lopsided tender smile that never failed to stir her curved at his lips. "I swear to you that I'm not in the least bit sorry that old man Potter messed things up and made you my wife."

The sparkle in his eyes telegraphed he wasn't the least bit remorseful about the promises he'd already broken, either. And, now that she took the time to think about it, neither was she. Angry or not. If only she could feel he wasn't going to be moved to turn into Stacey's knight in shining armor and come to the aid of a damsel in distress. He was that kind of a man. Maybe that was another reason she loved him so.

"One thing more, sweetheart," he said as he lightly kissed his way from her lips to her chin and down to the hollow between her breasts. "It may be the wrong time to tell you, but Stacey has to hide somewhere until we figure out a way to help her. Is it okay with you if she stays here with us for a while?''

"Of course," she whispered, ashamed of the pang of jealousy and the renewed doubts that came over her. Decency and her strong sense of guilt demanded she agree, but Jon's loyalty to Stacey stirred her misgivings. If Stacey was in real danger and it came down to saving her life, what would he do if it actually became a matter of choosing to help Stacey and her baby or their own life together?

"I'll see that she keeps out of sight until this is all over, sweetheart. She can sleep upstairs in the bedroom next to Belinda's."

"Okay." Hesitantly she touched the hair at the nape of his neck as he bent over her. He couldn't help his innate nobility. It was, after all, one of the things she loved about him. She'd have to see them through this mess.

As if on cue, they heard Belinda calling from outside the bedroom door. The doorknob rattled.

"It looks as if we'd better put the rest of this discussion on hold," she whispered with an impish smile. "We may have to finish clearing up this misunderstanding, but first things first, as my father always said."

"I have to talk to Belinda," he said, and sighed. "And it's about time I tell Stacey a few hard truths. As for getting the two of them together, I'm afraid we're too late. I'm willing to bet that they've already met!"

He rose and lifted Alex to his chest. "I never got around to changing my wet clothes, after all. Now," he whispered into her ear, "I don't need to. After a few minutes with you, these are bone-dry."

"And the hot shower?"

"That's another promise I intend to honor," he whispered as he gazed into her shadowed eyes. "I'll take a rain check until we're alone. And then, Mrs. Waring, you can expect me to deliver."

He thought she'd never looked so tempting.

"Are you ready to die with your boots on?" he asked in a stage whisper as he unlocked the bedroom door.

"I can hardly wait."

"Promises, promises!"

An apprehensive Belinda lingered outside the door. "There's someone waiting for you in the parlor, Uncle Jon," she whispered.

"I know, partner." He cast an apologetic glance at Alex and put his arm around Belinda's shoulder. A tomboy to the core, she smelled of horse, green grass and sunshine. Alexandra was going to have a devil of a hard time turning her into a lady, or he missed his guess. "Did you have fun riding out with the boys?"

"Sure, but..." She looked back over her shoulder. "Who *is* that lady?"

"Someone you said you wished was here. By any chance, did you introduce yourself?"

"Gosh, no!"

"Come on, then. You, too, Alexandra. Since it looks as if we're all going to have to live together in the same house for a while, let's get the introductions over. And then," he said, holding his hand to his stomach, "maybe we can have some of that stew

Cookie brought up while you were in the shower. I'm still starving."

Stacey got to her feet when Jon, Belinda and Alex joined her. She took a hesitant step toward Alex before they could speak. "I feel I should apologize to you for being so rude when we first met, Alexandra. I had no idea that you and Jon were actually husband and wife. Not that that excuses my rudeness, but..."

Alex swiftly moved to her side. Stacey had come to the ranch seeking shelter and she intended to help her find it. No matter how much she feared Jon and Stacey's longtime relationship might affect her own. There was a baby to consider. Stacey's genuine sincerity and the anguish in her eyes affected Alex deeply.

"Please don't apologize. I probably would have reacted the same way if I'd come back to find Jon had married someone else. Especially since you've gone to so much trouble to help him."

"Thank you. I would like us to be friends." Stacey turned to Jon and the young girl regarding her with wide eyes. "And this must be Belinda."

"Right." Jon pulled the silent girl forward. "B.J., this is Stacey Arden. You remember we talked about Stacey, don't you?" A teasing smile came to his lips as her complexion turned red. Without waiting for her to gather her composure, he went on, "Stacey, this is Belinda Joan, sometimes known as B.J."

Stacey felt a pang of remorse as she regarded the solemn girl. Until now, she'd never really thought of Belinda as a real person. The marriage, and then the proxy scheme to fool the courts had almost seemed like a game. She'd agreed only because she'd wanted to help Jon and, until Faoud had come back into her life, because she believed she had no love of her own waiting for her.

"I'm happy to meet you at last, B.J." Stacey smiled warmly. "I'm sorry I couldn't come through for you, but I'm sure you'll be happy with Alexandra."

Jon could feel the kid tense under his arm. Afraid that she might hurt Alexandra by revealing the depth of the way she actually felt about her, he broke into the conversation. "You certainly will, partner. You just wait and see."

"But what's Miss Burns gonna do when she finds both of them here?" B.J. blurted as she looked from Stacey to Alex. "She's gonna know we're not telling the truth!"

"Well, that *is* a problem we're going to have to face. But it wasn't exactly *not* telling the truth." Jon searched for a way to explain why he and Alex had had to pretend to be husband and wife even though it might be considered the wrong thing to do. He hated to admit he'd done anything illegal or morally wrong in front of B.J. He was supposed to be a role model for the kid, wasn't he?

"I did what I had to do in order to get a wife to satisfy the court." He regarded the three women solemnly watching him. "Now I'm going to have to come up with some kind of solution before Miss Burns gets here."

"Which one are you going to get rid of, Uncle Jon?"

Chapter Fourteen

Jon was prowling the kitchen making a pot of coffee when Alex joined him in the morning. Obviously worn-out from their rafting misadventure, she'd slept soundly all night. He hadn't had the heart to wake her. Not when he knew how little had been resolved between them.

"Hi, sleepyhead," he said cheerfully. "Ready for a new beginning?"

In the broad light of day, he noticed the uncertainty in her eyes. After B.J.'s question last night about whom to keep, her or Stacey, he didn't blame her. Nothing he'd said later to assure her he loved her and wanted her to stay with him and B.J. had seemed to make the difference.

Was it his relationship with Stacey that still bothered her? He'd tried to tell her Stacey was like a sister, a friend he had to protect. And while he intended to do just that, he'd hoped he made it clear he not only loved Alex but needed her. How much he did need her surprised the hell out of him. Life without her was unthinkable.

"Can we talk a minute?" Coffee could wait. He had more important things to take care of. He met her halfway, took her in his arms in spite of her half-hearted protests and, frustrated with the watchful look in her eyes, held her close. Her shoulders were soft and warm to the touch, but that spine of hers was stiff as a fence post.

"We need to talk," he said softly. "I guess I still haven't convinced you you've been my choice for my real wife for a long time."

"A long time?"

"Yes. From the day you fought off that steer with your bare hands. And later, when I held you in my arms at the Fourth of July dance and taught you how to two-step. There wasn't any choice at all, after that."

"But what about Stacey and B.J.?"

"I hope you're not upset over what B.J. said. Everything is going to be all right. I'm going to see to it."

"I wish I could afford to believe you, but I can't. I don't think there's much to be said that hasn't been said before." She tried to pull away from him. He held her closer.

"Talk to me, sweetheart," he said, kneading her shoulders. "I know there's something more bothering you. Actually, I was hoping you'd feel better about things this morning."

Her eyes locked with his. Finally she burst out, "Do you have any idea what it feels like to wait in the wings while someone else decides your future for you? No? Well, I do. Until I was twelve, I lived in a series of foster homes. I used to pray someone would want me enough to adopt me, that I would have a home and a family who loved me."

Tears came into her eyes. "I swore I would never let that happen to me again, and yet, I have, twice. Five years ago when my fiancé decided he didn't want me. And now, there's this thing with Stacey."

"But it's you I need and want." He held her face between his hands and kissed a tear away. "I don't know how you can doubt it. Your future is here, with me and B.J. I thought I've shown you that. Oh, Alexandra, give me a chance to prove it to you." He gazed deeply into her eyes, hoping that she could see how much he cared about her. It was no use, her flesh was cold, her voice firm as she took his hands away.

"Not until Stacey and her problem are taken care of. No, let me finish," she said when he started to protest. "I know you think you've made your choice. But I also know she has to come first with you because of the baby—no matter how hard you try not to admit that's the case, even to yourself. And, that's only right, considering the fine man you are. It's the waiting while you make up your mind to divorce me and marry her that tears me in two. Whatever you decide, decide it now. I can't take it any more." With a gesture of hopelessness, she turned her face away.

"I'm sorry I haven't been able to convince you. What do you want me to say? What do you want me to do before you believe me?"

"There's nothing you can say or do. Not while Stacey needs your protection."

"Alexandra . . . ?

"No, don't say anything more. I'd never ask you to make a choice between us. But," she added, "even all that isn't as important as Belinda."

"A choice? Alexandra, you're my hope for the future, the glue I've come to depend on to hold my life together. Far from being a mistake, our accidental marriage has been the luckiest thing that has ever happened to me."

"If only—"

"Hush. I said everything's going to come out all right and I meant it. You'll see," he said, tucking her head beneath his chin and absently stroking her damp cheek. "Trust me."

He could feel the heavy beat of her heart, the choke of her breath as she leaned into him. He knew he'd failed once again to convince her.

"God, I love you so much." He rested his chin on her curly brown hair and inhaled her fresh, sweet scent. "I wish things hadn't happened this way." Defeated, he sighed when she didn't answer.

"I've been thinking about where to hide Stacey," he went on. "As a matter of fact, I was going over to the bunkhouse to talk with Rusty about fixing up the line cabin for her. By the time we get through with it, it'll be a great place for her to hide out until after Burns drops in."

"Can't she go home to New York?" Alex questioned as she reluctantly moved out of his arms and wiped her eyes with the back of her hand.

"Unfortunately, no." With a shrug, he went back to wrestle with the coffee can. "From what she told me, her New York apartment apparently isn't the safest place for her to be right now. She still asleep?''

"I think so." Alex tried to pull herself together. Jon's plans for Stacey wouldn't change anything, nor would his lovemaking. It all came down to the fact that Stacey needed him to help her out of a terrible mess. There was no one else. When Jon realized he was her only hope, he would help her, even if he wasn't ready to face it yet. And there was Belinda. She needed him, too. And as for herself, she had no right to deny them that help.

Doubts about her own future with him grew stronger no matter how hard she tried to believe in him. In spite of everything he'd said, she was afraid to put her trust, her future, in his hands.

"She must be exhausted. I imagine she needs all the rest she can get. Here, let me," she said, taking the can of ground coffee he was struggling to open. He handed her the manual can opener. She measured the dark coffee into the pot and set it to brew.

Jon inhaled the strong scent and sighed. "I sure could use that coffee. Make it strong." He hid a yawn behind his hand and looked longingly at the refrigerator. "I'm hungry, too. Cookie tried to feed me earlier, but I wanted to get back in time for breakfast and to make sure the kid behaved this morning. Do you know where she is?"

"Good luck! She left through the front door as I was coming down the hall a few minutes ago. I saw her head for the barn." Alex rummaged in the refrigerator. "Bacon and eggs okay with you? Good. I'll have breakfast started in a minute. By the way, a line cabin doesn't sound like the place Stacey ought to stay in alone. Just what is a line cabin anyway?''

"Here, let me help you," he said as she juggled a butter dish, a package of bacon and a bowl of eggs. "It's a cabin close to the boundary line of Blue Sky and the next ranch. The men use it when they're out rounding up cattle. Since we don't have any fences except the one along the highway, the men have to guide the cattle that have strayed to our side back across the property line."

Alex looked doubtful. "Sounds pretty isolated. I don't see how you can expect Stacey to stay there, especially alone and pregnant."

"I never thought about that," he said with a sheepish grin. "Shows you how much I know about women and babies. I suppose you could be right." He opened the refrigerator, took out the orange juice and poured himself a glass. "I'll have to think of something else. In the meantime, I'd better move her car out of sight as soon as breakfast is over. Coffee ready?"

She poured him a cup and set about preparing breakfast. In passing, she glanced out of the kitchen window. Belinda was coming out of the barn cuddling the runt of the litter with the remainder of the puppies sliding at her heels. It took Alex only a few seconds to decide what to do.

"Here you are." She set his breakfast on the table. "Go ahead and eat, don't wait for me. I'll be back in a few minutes."

"Not hungry?" he asked. "I was looking forward to having a nice, peaceful breakfast. Just the two of us."

"Starved, but I bet I know a few puppies who are probably hungrier than I am. And someone I need to talk to." She took a large scoop of scrambled eggs left in the frying pan and reached to take two bowls out of the cupboard. "I've some fence-mending to do."

Belinda scowled when she saw Alex approach.

"I brought you some scrambled eggs in case you want to feed the puppies. Or has their mother come back?"

"No," Belinda replied shortly, glancing over at the barn. "She's not around. Guess some critter got a hold of her."

"Then, I guess you'll have to be their foster mother, won't you?" Alex mashed the eggs in one of the bowls and set it on the ground. She stood aside as the puppies tumbled over themselves in a rush to get to the food. "Here," she said, laughing at their antics when she put a small amount of egg in the other bowl. "Why don't you take care of the rest of the gang and I'll give that little guy his breakfast. He looks too small to compete with his brothers and sisters."

She watched while Belinda knelt down and busied herself feeding the animals. From her silence, Alex realized she'd have to make the next move or they'd never get off first base. So much hinged on their being friends, at least. "They certainly are lucky to have you to love them and take care of them," Alex said as she retrieved a tiny puppy at the rear of the pack struggling to get its share.

"Come on, big fella, I have breakfast for you, too." She sat down on a tree stump and watched the puppies fall over themselves as they frantically gobbled up the eggs. "They look too young to fend for themselves."

"Someone has to do it. They don't have their mother anymore," Belinda rejoined, her face hidden and her shoulders slumped as she bent over the puppies.

Alex realized Belinda felt the loss of her own parents more than she let on. Thoughtfully she dipped her finger into the eggs and rubbed it across the tiny puppy's mouth. She was rewarded by a minuscule pink tongue licking her fingers.

"Belinda, hasn't it occurred to you that I'm here for you, just as you are for the puppies?"

"That's different." Belinda's brown eyes were a mixture of defiance and pain as she gazed up at Alex. "I'm doing this because I really want to. Uncle Jon only hired you to act like you're his wife and to *pretend* you want to take care of us. Besides," she said with a sidelong look at Alex, "maybe Uncle Jon will choose Stacey."

Thunderstruck at Belinda's assessment of the situation, Alex could only stare at her. She should have realized the rebellious girl wasn't really a hellion, after all. She was an uncertain young girl not yet in tune with her emotions. Perhaps even jealous of another woman taking Jon's attention away and afraid of her position in his life if a new wife came into it. And too young to understand you can't buy someone else's love. Especially, a mother's love.

Her heart went out to the angry child. Belinda's parents hadn't been gone too long. It was obvious she was still searching for emotional security to take their place.

"Belinda, honey, you're dead wrong." Alex wanted to take the girl in her arms, but was hesitant to touch her for fear of shattering the sensitive moment. She had to reach her in another way. "I've never told you that I'm an adopted child myself, have I?"

"You are?"

She was relieved when Belinda risked a cautious glance at her instead of turning away. She'd struck a chord the girl understood. She watched as the yawning puppies finally curled up contentedly in Belinda's lap, and as, one by one, they fell asleep.

"Yes, I am. And just about your age—a few months older. My own parents died in an automobile accident. At first, no one wanted to adopt me, not even the few blood relatives I had in the world. Maybe it was because I was too old, ten. Or, maybe it was because my relatives were poor and none of them could afford to raise me."

She gazed down at the little runt fast asleep in her arms. Poor little guy, his mother was gone but at least they were here for him. "Anyway, I'd lived in foster homes for a few years when my new parents found me. They were too old to adopt an infant, and it seemed I suited them just fine."

Belinda's troubled eyes widened as she considered Alex. "I have a cousin in New York who doesn't want me, either," she said after a moment's consideration. "That was okay with me," she said with a defiant toss of her brown curls. "At first the judge said he'd have to take me, but Uncle Jon insisted he wanted me more.''

"You're lucky. I was lucky, too." Alex smiled at the recollection of the happiness reflected in the faces of her new parents when the adoption papers were finally signed. And of the joy in her own heart.

"I want you to know your uncle could never pay me enough to do something I didn't want to do. I didn't realize it at the time, but I've loved your uncle almost from the moment I met him."

Belinda didn't look convinced. Of course, Alex realized, the girl probably didn't relate to that line of reasoning. She went on. "Actually though, it wasn't until he told me about you, that I agreed to come here with him. I wanted you to be as happy as I was when my parents picked me. I know I can never take the place of your own mother, but I want to help you. Love has nothing to do with money."

It had been true, Alex reflected. She *had* agreed only after Jon had mentioned the problem with Belinda's adoption and insisted she take the money she so obviously needed. But she couldn't ignore the way she felt about Jon. Not then, nor now. He was a mixture of all the things she'd dreamed of in a husband: thoughtful, caring, kind, responsible and dependable. And every moment he held her in his powerful arms and made love to her was unforgettable.

She knew he would never leave her for just any another woman. But for Stacey and her baby? That was an entirely different matter.

"You did? You came because of me?" A reluctant Belinda glanced up at Alex. Admitting she'd behaved badly was obviously something hard for her to do. That Alex understood. She wasn't going to ask for anything more than the girl could give.

"Can we at least try to be friends?" Alex held out a hand for Belinda to shake.

"I guess so." An uncertain smile on her face, Belinda finally dislodged a sleeping puppy from her lap, wiped her hands on her jeans and shook hands. "You're not mad at me for acting like a jerk?"

"Not at all. Good, we're friends then. And together we'll help Stacey get through the next few weeks," Alex said with a conspiratorial smile. "We women have to stick together, don't we?"

A broad grin broke over Belinda's face. "Cool," she said. "Yeah, we women have to stick together."

"SHE'S HERE, Uncle Jon!" Belinda announced breathlessly as she dashed into the kitchen. "I saw Miss Burns's car coming up the road."

"Well, my wish has come true sooner than I expected, thank God. Now maybe we can relax and get on with our lives." Secure in the knowledge that Stacey was asleep upstairs, Jon made a quick inventory of the room. They had to look as if it were a normal day if they were going to convince Letty Burns that they had settled down to being a happy family. He took a seat and motioned to Alex.

She hurriedly put steaming platters of ham and eggs, toast and a pitcher of milk on the table. "Now we're ready."

"Good. We're going to have to play this out very carefully. Burns is no dummy." He cast a stern look at

Belinda. "Not a word about Stacey, you hear? And no matter what Miss Burns has to say, I want you to let me handle it."

"I promise, Uncle Jon. Cross my heart and hope to die."

"You don't have to go that far, partner." He laughed uneasily, and he prayed that today was going to be a good one for a change. "Remember, this is supposed to be an ordinary morning in the life of an ordinary family."

Like hell it is, he added to himself when he heard a strong knock on the door. There was nothing ordinary about them. Alex looked like an automated doll, B.J. was acting as if she were sitting on a prickly pear. As for him, he kept listening for the turning of that damned wagon wheel.

"Ah, good morning, Miss Burns," he said as he opened the screen door and led her into the kitchen. "What a surprise. You're in time for breakfast."

"Just coffee, thanks." Letty Burns nodded her greeting as Jon pulled out a chair for her. "I told you I'd be dropping by occasionally. Though I do apologize for coming so early. I have a heavy caseload today." She accepted a cup of coffee, sat back in her seat and surveyed the watching trio. "Well, how have you folks been getting along?"

"Just fine, thanks." Jon waved his fork at Belinda. "Alexandra's settled in and she and B.J. have really hit it off. Not only that, the kid has made an adoption of her own—a family of puppies."

"Belinda?" Letty Burn's inquiring gaze swung to the girl. "That's a big responsibility. Are you sure you can handle it?"

"Yes, ma'am. The puppies lost their mother, so I'm taking care of them. And Aunt Alex is helping me. We women have to stick together, you know."

Alex had trouble keeping a straight face. When Miss Burns turned her questioning gaze on her, Alex nodded. "We certainly do," she said with a telling look at the woman. She was rewarded when a faint smile came over the caseworker's face.

"Yes, I guess we do," Miss Burns responded faintly.

Everything looked to be going well, Jon thought. In fact, it was the only time he could remember seeing Burns smile. Maybe this day *was* going to be a good one.

"Good morning, everyone!"

Maybe not. Stacey had awakened.

Stacey's voice fell away when she entered the kitchen and noticed their visitor. "Oh, hi, Letty. I didn't expect to see you here."

Letty Burns turned a questioning glare at Jon. "Well, good morning, Stacey. I understood you were in Europe and that you weren't expected anytime soon."

"Oh, that!" Stacey laughed, uneasy now that she saw the frown on Jon's face and the wide-eyed look on Belinda's. "You know how unpredictable the news business is."

"You're looking well," Letty said. "Although there *is* something different about you." Her eyes raked Stacey from head to toe, narrowing as she took in her pale face and slightly rounded belly. She absently accepted the refilled cup of coffee Alex handed her. "Could you possibly be expecting?"

Jon blanched as Letty Burns turned her gaze on him. Beside him, he heard Alex muffle a groan. There was no doubt in his mind what Burns thought. He tried a noncommittal smile. It looked to him as if all his plans were going to be blown in bits and pieces, and that the adoption of B.J. might go with them.

"Well, yes." Stacey fell into a chair at the table and glanced over to Jon, who was making eye signals for her to be careful. It was too late. "I wanted to keep it quiet for a while, Letty. I hope you understand."

"I can imagine that you would." She emptied her cup of coffee and set it aside. "This certainly complicates things, doesn't it?" She looked accusingly at Jon.

"I don't know why," Jon countered, thinking rapidly. How could he protect Stacey's secret and not give away his own? "Stacey's pregnancy has nothing to do with my marriage to Alex and the adoption proceedings."

"I believe it does." She paused for effect. "Mr. Waring, before we discuss this any further, I think Belinda should be excused. This is not a subject fit for an impressionable young girl."

Belinda looked at her uncle and jumped to her feet when he nodded his head.

"Why don't you go check on the puppies, partner?"

He waited until B.J. disappeared through the kitchen door. When he was certain she couldn't hear what they were saying, he fixed a cold stare on their questioner.

"Just what is it about Stacey's pregnancy that seems to bother you so much, Miss Burns?"

"It should be obvious, Mr. Waring. Since I happen to know how close you and Stacey have been. There's no doubt in my mind who's the father of her child. The shame of it all is that you're married to another woman!"

Chapter Fifteen

If ever a man needed a lucky break, Jon thought with a sinking feeling, it was him. And he needed it now. Praying for a miracle, he knew he had to give Burns some explanation. At least enough to satisfy her. He put a warning hand on Stacey's arm and forced himself to meet her eyes with a bland expression.

"Just what do I need to do to convince you I am *not* the father of Stacey's baby?"

"Come now, Mr. Waring. Not too long ago, when she and I were working together, Stacey told me you'd been engaged at one time. It seems only logical to believe you've fathered her baby. What I don't understand," she said firmly, "is why you would marry someone else instead of accepting the responsibility of fatherhood as you profess to want with Belinda."

"I thought I explained that Alexandra and I fell in love, almost from first sight."

"That may be the case in fairy tales, sir. It seldom happens in real life. And now that we've come down to the truth, I have a strong feeling your marriage to

Alexandra Storm may be a sham, perpetrated to comply with the court's wishes.''

The events of the past two weeks ran through Jon's mind. Had he said or done anything to give himself away? Had Alex? B.J.? He couldn't recall a single instance.

Miss Letty Burns was smarter than he'd believed.

He decided to give the lady a bare-bones explanation. Hopefully, she had an open mind and a heart warmer than the expression on her face.

He was interrupted when the telephone rang.

Jon breathed a sigh of relief. Any interruption was welcome. He excused himself and went to answer the phone. ''Jon Waring.''

A heavily accented voice answered. ''Mr. Waring, you may not know me, but my name is Faoud. I'll skip the last name for now, if you don't mind. I'm a friend of a close friend of yours.''

''And?'' Jon questioned warily, glancing over his shoulder and motioning for quiet.

''*Have* you heard of me, Mr. Waring?''

''You might say so.'' Jon tried to be noncommittal, but there was no doubt in his mind as to the identity of his caller.

''Good. I am able to tell you I'm in Bern, Switzerland. I have just received political amnesty through the American embassy and have applied for permission to come to your country.''

''That's a dangerous game you're playing, Mr. . . .''

''More dangerous than perhaps even I know. I was not able to call you before now. However, I will tell you that the government of my country is in danger and may be about to fall. And before there are complications, I hope to be on my way to the United States."

"That's all very interesting." Jon tried to be non-committal. The caller could have been anyone. "Just what do you think I can do for you?" He didn't want to give Stacey's presence away until he was certain the caller was her lover.

"Please tell your friend that things have eased and I hope to join her in a few days . . . that is, if you will extend me the courtesy of allowing me to join you?"

"Call again when you hit the States." His mind spinning with the need for caution, Jon stalled for time. "We'll talk again."

After a short farewell and promises to pass on his message, he hung up and went back to the table where Letty Burns was waiting. "Well," he said, trying to mask his elation. He didn't want to have Stacey's heart broken if things didn't turn out the way they were planned. "Unless I'm mistaken, Stacey, I think your lucky number has just turned up. But don't get your hopes up too high. Give it some time."

"And just what is that supposed to mean?" Letty Burns took in the openmouthed trio.

"Simply put," Stacey said as she hugged herself, "it may mean that the father of my child is coming for me, Letty."

"Are you saying Mr. Waring is not the father of your child?"

"No, he's not."

"Well," Miss Burns said, thoughtfully gazing at Jon. "I can't remember a case as complicated as this one. But at least, it looks as if might have a happy ending. Now, as to your own marriage, Mr. Waring. Can you assure me that you intend to make a good home for Belinda? And that you'll remain married to your wife?"

"I promise." He saw Alex raise a doubting eyebrow. "Don't you ever doubt it," he said as much to her as to Miss Burns.

Belinda came cautiously into the kitchen carrying a puppy in her arms. "Is it all right to come in now? Tiger needs something to eat."

"Tiger? You named that runt Tiger?" Jon studied the small puppy as its pink tongue licked B.J.'s face. "I can't think of a less likely name. He looks as if a strong wind would blow him over." He turned to Miss Burns. "I hope we've satisfied all your concerns."

"Well, it does look as if Belinda is a lucky girl in having you and your wife as new parents. Now that that's settled, I'm sure I can in good conscience close the case," Letty Burns said as she gathered her purse and papers. She looked Jon meaningfully in the eyes. "Sometimes plans turn out better than originally intended, don't they? And you, Stacey, I wish you well."

Jon had the strangest feeling they hadn't fooled Burns for a minute.

"WELL, SWEETHEART," he said later when Stacey, Belinda and Tiger finally went upstairs for the night, "there's just the two of us now. It looks as if we can get on with that honeymoon."

Alex could hardly wait, but the events of the past few days had finally caught up with her. "I don't know about that. I'm so worn-out I can hardly wait to get to bed.''

''Me, too.'' Jon cast a speculative eye at his wife. A protective feeling came over him as he noted her half-closed eyes. Until he'd witnessed her exhaustion, he'd been planning a real honeymoon celebration. Including that shared hot shower he'd promised her. Well, he thought philosophically, at least he'd be able to hold her all through the night. And he'd be there when she awakened in the morning.

He swept her into his arms and carried her into the bedroom. She murmured her apologies as he undressed her, garment by garment, until her warm, silken skin was exposed to his loving gaze. She felt like velvet under his fingers: he wanted to touch her everywhere, to make her body sing in consonance with his.

He wished she was awake so he could tell her how much he loved her, how much a part of him she'd become. That there were no longer choices to be made, no bridges to burn. He shuddered to think how close he'd come to losing her before the wheel of life had turned once again and made her his forever.

He undressed, slid into bed beside her and rested his arms behind his head, remembering, thinking, wishing. He'd resigned himself to a sleepless night when he heard her whisper his name.

''Is that how you keep your promises?'' a soft voice whispered in his ear. ''Aren't you going to make love to me?''

"Before or after the shower?" he said as he turned into her arms. Even in darkness he could make out the smile on her face, the sparkle in her eyes.

She dropped her head on his chest. "Both," she said softly. "That is, if you think you have the stamina."

"I thought you were too tired, but if you're up to it, I'll show you stamina, woman. I promise you won't want to leave this bed."

"Not ever?"

"Not ever." She spied a wicked grin on his face before he buried his lips in the sensitive part of her neck. "Or at least until you beg for mercy."

Alex held him to her and stroked the curls at his nape. "Never," she whispered as she slid her hands down his back to his tight rear. "Not even when the honeymoon is over."

His body convulsed at her touch. He had to close his eyes and concentrate on the question at hand or the honeymoon would be over before it began. "It's never going to be over. Not if I can help it. Did I ever tell you how much I love you?" he asked as he leaned back and looked down at her.

"I don't remember," she said, pulling him to her. "Tell me again."

"I love you," he said as he kissed her shining eyes, held her close and worshiped her body, her sweet soul. He would never have enough of her, never run out of things to talk about with her. Not even if they lived together for fifty years.

"I don't know how I could have been so stupid all these years not to realize that when I thought everyone needed me, it was because I needed them, too.

You've shown me that, sweetheart. You and B.J. Thank God for the both of you." He kissed his way down her body. "I feel as if I'm the luckiest man in the world."

"And I'm the luckiest woman."

At a slight pressure from his knee, Alex opened to him. When he joined his body to hers, she felt as though she had dived into a warm, blue lake and the water was closing over her, taking her deeper and deeper into an erotic world. She drifted in its depths, floated in a tide of heightened sensations.

She was his forever, she thought as she strained to be even closer to him. She couldn't get enough of the male scent of him, the feel of his muscular arms around her, his firm body over her. She returned his kiss, tasted the warmth of his mouth.

"I love you," she whispered into his lips. "This has to be the luckiest mistake ever made."

Epilogue

"All's well that ends well," Alex commented as they watched the black sedan carrying Stacey and her new husband fade out of sight. "I'd never really believed in fairy-tale endings before, but I do now."

"And here's to new beginnings, my sweet Alexandra," Jon said as he took her hand in his and turned her around to face him. "Now that the secret is not a secret anymore, you can even write your story now. That is, if you still want to."

She shook her head. "I don't want to. I'm too busy living it."

"As a matter of fact, sweetheart," he said when he was through kissing her, "I think we should make this a real beginning for us, too." At her questioning look, he smiled. "I'd feel foolish getting down on bended knee here in the dirt, but I have a question to ask you. Will you marry me?"

"Idiot!" She laughed and stroked a lock of hair away from his eyes. "We're already married."

A sheepish look flitted across Jon's face, and his gaze wavered. "Jon," she called. "Look at me. What is it?'' When he did, he looked like the proverbial cat who ate the canary. "Jon, it can't be that bad.''

He swallowed. "Well...that's just it. We may not be married...''

"What!''

"Potter called the other day while you were shopping with Stacey and B.J.''

"Potter called you? I'm surprised he could remember your name. What did he want?''

"Said he felt bad about the mistake he made. And that Judge Simmons has changed his ruling. We may not be married, after all. He wanted to know if we needed any help with another marriage ceremony or, possibly, an annulment.''

Shocked, Alex didn't know whether to laugh or cry. Finally, she opted for the former. "Not with Potter, bless him,'' she said through chuckles. "I'm grateful to him but I don't think I could go through all of this again.''

Jon looked relieved at her reaction. "But the fact is, we only fell into marriage, with his help. I want you to marry me in a church with all the trimmings and because you want to.'' He stood and took her in his arms. "What do you say?''

"You can't be serious. Everyone will think we're crazy!''

"Let them. So tell me, will you marry me?''

Alex gazed into his laughing green eyes and saw her future there. A home, a husband and, with luck, more children to keep Belinda company. She looked over her shoulder to where the girl was kneeling on the ground surrounded by the litter of gamboling puppies. "Belinda?"

"Yes, Aunt Alex?"

"How would you like to be a maid of honor?"

"Cool! Who's getting married?"

"Your uncle and I."

"Wow! Can I have a real bridesmaid's dress?"

"You bet. As frilly as they come."

Two weeks later, the mistake became a real marriage, after all.

BRIDE'S BAY RESORT

UNLOCK THE DOOR TO GREAT ROMANCE AT BRIDE'S BAY RESORT

Join Harlequin's new across-the-lines series, set in an exclusive hotel on an island off the coast of South Carolina.

Seven of your favorite authors will bring you exciting stories about fascinating heroes and heroines discovering love at Bride's Bay Resort.

Look for these fabulous stories coming to a store near you beginning in January 1996.

Harlequin American Romance #613 in January
Matchmaking Baby by Cathy Gillen Thacker

Harlequin Presents #1794 in February
Indiscretions by Robyn Donald

Harlequin Intrigue #362 in March
Love and Lies by Dawn Stewardson

Harlequin Romance #3404 in April
Make Believe Engagement by Day Leclaire

Harlequin Temptation #588 in May
Stranger in the Night by Roseanne Williams

Harlequin Superromance #695 in June
Married to a Stranger by Connie Bennett

Harlequin Historicals #324 in July
Dulcie's Gift by Ruth Langan

Visit Bride's Bay Resort each month wherever Harlequin books are sold.

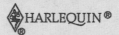

HARLEQUIN ®

BBAYG

MILLION DOLLAR SWEEPSTAKES (III)

No purchase necessary. To enter, follow the directions published. Method of entry may vary. For eligibility, entries must be received no later than March 31, 1996. No liability is assumed for printing errors, lost, late or misdirected entries. Odds of winning are determined by the number of eligible entries distributed and received. Prizewinners will be determined no later than June 30, 1996.

Sweepstakes open to residents of the U.S. (except Puerto Rico), Canada, Europe and Taiwan who are 18 years of age or older. All applicable laws and regulations apply. Sweepstakes offer void wherever prohibited by law. Values of all prizes are in U.S. currency. This sweepstakes is presented by Torstar Corp., its subsidiaries and affiliates, in conjunction with book, merchandise and/or product offerings. For a copy of the Official Rules send a self-addressed, stamped envelope (WA residents need not affix return postage) to: MILLION DOLLAR SWEEPSTAKES (III) Rules, P.O. Box 4573, Blair, NE 68009, USA.

EXTRA BONUS PRIZE DRAWING

No purchase necessary. The Extra Bonus Prize will be awarded in a random drawing to be conducted no later than 5/30/96 from among all entries received. To qualify, entries must be received by 3/31/96 and comply with published directions. Drawing open to residents of the U.S. (except Puerto Rico), Canada, Europe and Taiwan who are 18 years of age or older. All applicable laws and regulations apply; offer void wherever prohibited by law. Odds of winning are dependent upon number of eligibile entries received. Prize is valued in U.S. currency. The offer is presented by Torstar Corp., its subsidiaries and affiliates in conjunction with book, merchandise and/or product offering. For a copy of the Official Rules governing this sweepstakes, send a self-addressed, stamped envelope (WA residents need not affix return postage) to: Extra Bonus Prize Drawing Rules, P.O. Box 4590, Blair, NE 68009, USA.

SWP-H1295

IT'S A BABY BOOM!

NEW ARRIVALS

We're expecting—again! Join us for the New Arrivals promotion, in which special American Romance authors invite you to read about equally special heroines—all of whom are on a nine-month adventure! We expect each mom-to-be will find the man of her dreams—and a daddy in the bargain!

Watch for the newest arrival. Due date: next month...

#617 THE BOUNTY HUNTER'S BABY
by Jule McBride
February 1996

What do women really want to know?

Only the world's largest publisher of romance
fiction could possibly attempt an answer.

HARLEQUIN ULTIMATE GUIDES™

How to Talk to a Naked Man,

Make the Most of Your Love Life,
and Live Happily Ever After

The editors of Harlequin and Silhouette are
definitely experts on love, men and relationships.
And now they're ready to share that expertise with
women everywhere.

Jam-packed with vital, indispensable, lighthearted
tips to improve every area of your romantic life—even
how to get one! So don't just sit around and wonder
why, how or where—run to your nearest bookstore
for your copy now!

Available this February, at your favorite retail outlet.

HARLEQUIN®
AMERICAN ◆ ROMANCE®

This Valentine's Day, take your pick of the four extraspecial heroes who are coming your way. Or why not take *all* of them?

Four of the most fearless, strong and sexy men are brought to their knees by the undeniable power of love. And it all happens next month in

Valentine's MEN

Don't miss any of these:

#617 THE BOUNTY HUNTER'S BABY
by Jule McBride

#618 THE COWBOY AND THE CENTERFOLD
by Debbi Rawlins

#619 FLYBOY
by Rosemary Grace

#620 THE BEWITCHING BACHELOR
by Charlotte Maclay

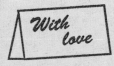

With love From HARLEQUIN AMERICAN ROMANCE

Are your lips succulent, impetuous, delicious or racy?

Find out in a very special Valentine's Day promotion—THAT SPECIAL KISS!

Inside four special Harlequin and Silhouette February books are details for THAT SPECIAL KISS! explaining how you can have your lip prints read by a romance expert.

Look for details in the following series books, written by four of Harlequin and Silhouette readers' favorite authors:

Silhouette Intimate Moments #691
Mackenzie's Pleasure by *New York Times* bestselling author Linda Howard

Harlequin Romance #3395
Because of the Baby by Debbie Macomber

Silhouette Desire #979
Megan's Marriage by Annette Broadrick

Harlequin Presents #1793
The One and Only by Carole Mortimer

Fun, romance, four top-selling authors, plus a **FREE** gift! This is a very special Valentine's Day you won't want to miss! Only from Harlequin and Silhouette.

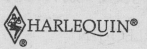 

VAL96

You're About to Become a
Privileged Woman

Reap the rewards of fabulous free gifts and
benefits with proofs-of-purchase from
Harlequin and Silhouette books

Pages & Privileges™

It's our way of thanking you for
buying our books at your
favorite retail stores.

PROOF OF PURCHASE
HAR-PP90
Offer expires October 31, 1996

**Harlequin and Silhouette—
the most privileged readers in the world!**

For more information about Harlequin and
Silhouette's PAGES & PRIVILEGES program call the
Pages & Privileges Benefits Desk: 1-503-794-2499

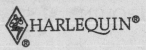

HARLEQUIN®

HAR-PP90